DOUBLE FELIX

Sally Harris

illustrated by Maria Serrano

Kane Miller

A DIVISION OF EDC PUBLISHING

First American Edition 2019
Kane Miller, A Division of EDC Publishing

First published in the UK in 2018 by Wacky Bee Books
Text © Sally Harris 2018
Illustrations © Maria Serrano 2018
The moral rights of the author and illustrator
have been asserted.

For information contact:
Kane Miller, A Division of EDC Publishing
PO Box 470663
Tulsa, OK 74147-0663
www.kanemiller.com
www.usbornebooksandmore.com
www.edcpub.com

Library of Congress Control Number: 2018958288
Printed and bound in the United States of America
1 2 3 4 5 6 7 8 9 10
ISBN: 978-1-61067-947-3

*"For all the students who kept asking me
'And then what happens?' until this book
was finished. Particularly you, Maddy.
Far out, you are persistent!"* – Sally Harris

*"To my parents. With thanks for all your
love and support"* – Maria Serrano

Contents

Two

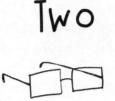

As far as I'm concerned, each day can be sorted into one of two categories:

A) A day that goes exactly as it should go and in a really good way; or

B) A day that goes another direction entirely and not in a really good way.

Today started off as an "A" day, but it seems to have taken a wrong turn toward being more of a "B" kind of day.

The reason I know this is because I am sitting in the principal's office when I should be in class. It's Monday, so I should be doing spelling because that is what we do first thing every Monday.

I've been in Mrs. Lovejoy's office before. This isn't the first time. I have actually spent quite a bit of time in here over the years I have been at Scribbly Gum Primary School. There have been a few ... well, a few misunderstandings.

But, today is different.

It is different because Mrs. Lovejoy isn't in here with me. I'm in here by myself. And the door is locked. With Mrs. Lovejoy on the outside. I don't think that she is very happy about this arrangement. I can tell because she is shouting. Mom told me that when people shout, they are usually upset about something.

I don't know why she is unhappy. I'm the one who should be upset. I'm the one who is locked in her office. I'm the one who is now having a very, very "B" for bad kind of day.

"Felix?" Mrs. Lovejoy calls loudly through the door. She is using her just-pretending-to-be-cheerful voice. It is high-pitched and singsong. "Can you open up, please?"

Mrs. Lovejoy doesn't need to shout. I can hear what she is saying perfectly well. It is a very thin door.

She rattles the handle; the door remains locked.

Then I hear her say more quietly, "Helen, get me a knife."

I think she might be talking to Mrs. Troy who sits at the front desk and makes announcements over the PA system. Mrs. Troy wears very pointy high heels that make a clip-clopping noise like a pony when she walks. I hear her push her chair back from her desk and trot her way down the hallway to the teachers' lounge.

"Felix? Are you OK in there?" Mrs. Lovejoy interrupts my thoughts. "Why don't you just open the door and we can talk about this sensibly?"

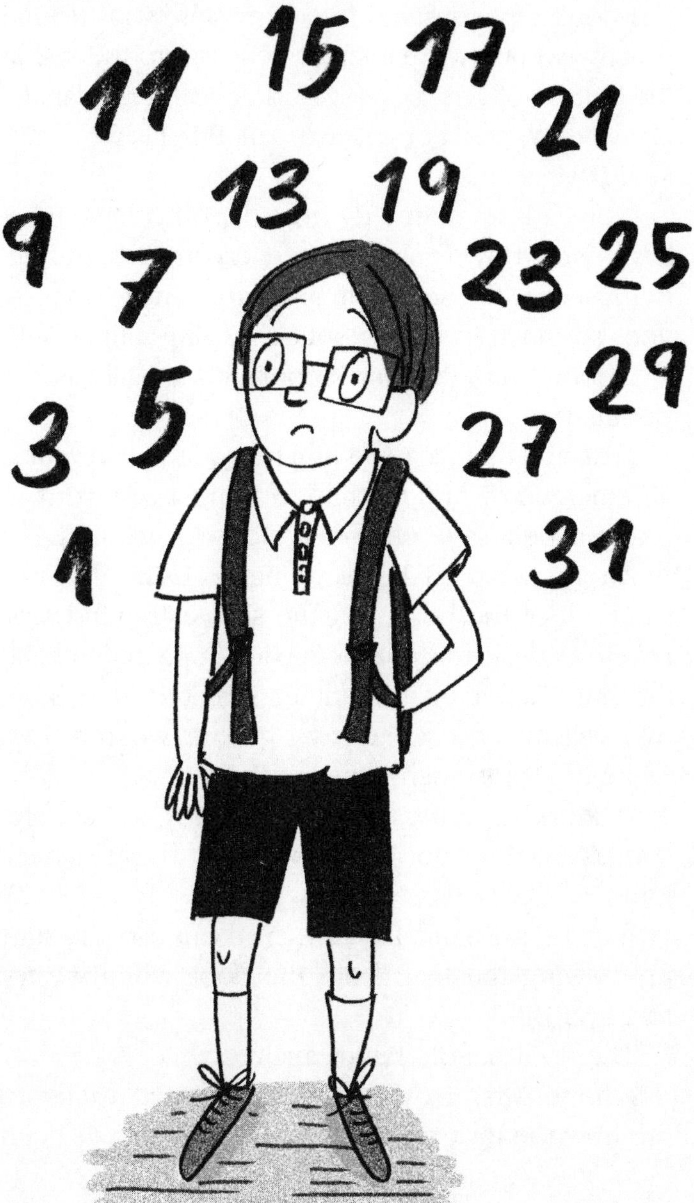

15
17
11
21
13
19
9
7
23
25
29
5
3
27
1
31

I don't reply. Instead I keep myself busy sticking exactly twenty-two pens and pencils into the soil at the bottom of Mrs. Lovejoy's fiddle leaf fern plant.

"Monica, can you please call Bill Fisher?" says Mrs. Lovejoy.

Monica is another lady from the office. She must have come down to see why everyone is shouting. Bill Fisher is the school maintenance man. Nobody does so much as think about changing a light bulb at Scribbly Gum Primary School without Bill Fisher's permission.

"Tell him that we need him here immediately. It is an emergency. And tell him to bring a screwdriver. And maybe a saw? Or an ax? Do we have an ax?"

An ax? What is she planning on using that for? I pull all of the books off the shelves behind Mrs. Lovejoy's desk and put them back in pairs that have the same color on the spine. Two red, two blue, two yellow, two white, two green, two red, two white. It looks much better now.

"I found a knife," I hear Mrs. Troy say, as she comes trotting noisily back from the teachers' lounge.

"Great," says Mrs. Lovejoy. "You can use it to start unscrewing the lock from the door while we try and find Bill."

The door handle rattles again.

I hope Mrs. Troy doesn't cut herself trying to unscrew the lock on the door. She has always been nice to me. She never complains when she has to call Mom to bring my lunch to school when I have forgotten it because I'm having a day that is going in the wrong direction.

"Felix! Open up!" shouts Mrs. Lovejoy again, knocking on her office door. She is starting to sound a bit less cheerful now.

I hear more footsteps then another voice joins the conversation. It sounds like Miss Jessup, who was my teacher last year. Miss Jessup was a nice teacher. I didn't seem to get into trouble nearly as much when I had Miss Jessup. I think it is because she stuck to the rules and when we were meant to do something, we did it. She would never have tried to teach science first thing on Monday when we are meant to be doing spelling.

There is another knock on the door and I hear Miss Jessup say, "Felix. Could you open the door for me, please? We are all worried about you out here."

I step up onto Mrs. Lovejoy's chair in order to reach the framed pictures on the wall. There are five of them clustered together in a group directly behind her desk, all created by students at the school and arranged in a jumbled bunch on the wall. There seems to be no order to them at all. I carefully remove the painting of a sleeping giraffe by Kayla C. in Room B and throw it, frame and all, into the trash can. I take down the other four frames and pull the nails out of the wall. Then,

using Mrs. Lovejoy's stapler like a hammer, I neatly bang the nails back into the wall in the correct place and rehang the four pictures in two groups of two.

"Maybe we should call his mother?" says Miss Jessup. "She'll be able to help."

"I've already called her. She should be here any minute," Mrs. Troy says, sighing and shaking the door handle. The door remains firmly locked.

I remove one of the three brightly patterned cushions that Mrs. Lovejoy has sitting on the armchairs in her office. Three cushions just won't do. I look around for a place to stash the extra cushion, but Mrs. Lovejoy really does have limited storage options in here. Then my eyes come to rest on the industrial-sized paper shredder behind her desk. I could get rid of it permanently for her. I place the cushion on top of the shredder, then I turn it on.

The blades of the shredder whir and the edge of the fancy fabric of the cushion begins to get chewed up by the machine.

"Felix! What is that noise?" calls Mrs. Lovejoy, over the noise of the paper shredder in action. She is definitely beginning to sound a bit panicked now.

Unfortunately, the entire cushion is too thick to actually fit through the paper shredder. The more fabric that disappears into the machine, the less space the feathers have left inside what is left of the cushion cover.

"Thank goodness you're here," I hear Mrs. Lovejoy say outside the door.

There is a jangling of keys, so I'm guessing that Bill Fisher has finally turned up. He has a big key ring that contains over one hundred keys, one for every room in the school and some that I don't think even he knows what they open.

"Now, let me see," I can hear him slowly trying a key in the lock. "No, it isn't that one." I can hear the chink of keys as he slides them around on the ring before trying another one in the lock. "Not that one either."

The paper shredder groans as it tries to chew up more of the cushion, but it's stuck. Very, very stuck.

I can hear him sorting through some keys before he tries another one. "No, it isn't that key either. Hmmm ... What about this one?"

He tries a fourth key in the lock. He seems to be working at the pace of a sloth. "Well, it definitely isn't that one," he comments.

The fabric stretches tight as the cogs of the paper shredder strain, trying desperately to continue pulling fabric into the machine, and the feathers are now squashed together so tightly in the fabric that they have nowhere else to go. The machine is making a noise like the motor might be about to die at any moment.

"Oh, just give them to me!" shrieks Mrs. Lovejoy. I hear her snatch the keys from Bill Fisher and begin trying key after key in the lock, rattling the handle each time as if one of them might miraculously open the door.

The paper shredder begins to shudder and large puffs of smoke begin to come out of the back.

A key turns in the lock and Mrs. Lovejoy bursts into the room just as the cushion cover can take the pressure no more. The seams of the fabric rip open and feathers explode into the air like a mushroom. They rain down from the ceiling and cover the room in a layer of white fluff. It looks just like snow.

Mrs. Lovejoy just stands there with her mouth hanging open. She is probably just so surprised by all of the improvements I have made to her office in the short time I have been in here.

We look at each other for a moment, both covered in feathers.

"Hello, Mrs. Lovejoy. Hello, Mrs. Lovejoy," I say.

Then it starts to rain.

This time it isn't raining feathers. It is raining water. Actual water. From the sprinklers on the ceiling meant to detect smoke and put out fires. Like I told you. Today is going badly.

And from the look on Mrs. Lovejoy's face, I think she agrees.

Four

After she stops ranting and raving about me being "completely out of control," Mrs. Lovejoy directs me to sit on the chair outside her office and instructs me not to move until Mom arrives to pick me up. As she says this, the pair of little white feathers that are stuck to her forehead quiver slightly. I slump into the striped armchair by the door and tap my fingers on the arm. One, two, one, two, one two.

Today started off as a good day. My morning went something like this.

Mom woke me up in the usual way, by standing in the doorway to the bedroom and saying "Good morning, Henry. Good morning, Felix."

And I replied just like I always do by saying "Good morning, Mom. Good morning, Mom."

My older brother Henry just grunted.

Before I got up, I counted the slats on the bunk bed that I share with Henry. Two, four, six, eight, ten, twelve. This made me happy because twelve is an even number and it is divisible by two, four and six, all of which are also even numbers. Even always means a good start to the day.

The next thing I did was to slide my legs out of bed so that my feet didn't touch the ground at the same time. Instead, I put them down carefully – one, then two.

"Good morning, Henry. Good morning, Henry," I called as I pulled on my bathrobe. Henry grunted again. He is a very grunty person. Maybe he is sick? Maybe he is dying? I decided that I'd better tell Mom.

I left Henry in bed. I jumped down the stairs, two at a time, and jumped twice on the spot when I landed at the bottom.

"Mom, Henry is dying," I told her, as I pulled myself up into my spot at the kitchen counter between my two sisters.

Alice, who is thirteen, was eating toast, tap dancing with her feet and listening to music so loud that we all heard it, even though she was wearing headphones. Lavender, who is seven, alternated between eating mouthfuls of cereal and putting pieces of it up her nose. This morning Mom had my bowl of cereal ready in just the right way. Spoon on the right, bowl filled with cereal up to the fourth line and milk in a cup next to it.

"Mom," I told her again, "Henry is absolutely dying."

Mom looked up at me from the other side of the counter where she was making sandwiches for lunch and trying not to squash The Bump into the countertop.

"Dying?" she asked me, eyebrows raised.

"Yes," I told her. "He is groaning. A lot. All the time. And he smells."

Mom chuckled. "I think what he has is a severe case of teenager, Felix. Every day he gets out of bed on the wrong side."

"That is impossible," I told her. "The left side of the bed is against the wall. He can only get in and out of the right side. Plus it is a bunk bed and he is on the top."

I then poured half of my milk into my bowl and

mixed the cereal around so that it all got an equal amount of the milk. Then I poured the other half of the milk in and stirred again.

"I guess you're right, Felix," Mom said, and sighed, like she often does. "In this case, when someone gets out on the wrong side of the bed, it's like saying that they are always in a bad mood."

I took a mouthful of cereal, chewed and thought about this for a moment.

"Why wouldn't you just say that someone is in a bad mood then?"

Mom sighed again and rubbed The Bump. I am really not happy about The Bump being here. The Bump is another baby that means there will be five children and seven people in our family altogether. This is bad news. Five is not a good number. Neither is seven. I think that we should just be four children and six in total if you count Mom and Dad. Plus, where will The Bump sit for breakfast? There aren't any more spots available at the kitchen counter.

Anyway, this morning, everything else at home went exactly as it should have. I finished my breakfast, had a shower for exactly two minutes, then I was out, dried and into my school uniform. Red T-shirt and blue shorts every day. R-e-d-a-n-d-b-l-u-e is an even number of letters and that means good. I would wear it on weekends too if I could. I like my uniform because it is always the right thing to wear to school. Not like on weekends when there is the risk of putting on the wrong thing. Like putting on a Spider-Man costume to go to swimming lessons is the wrong thing. I know that. Well, I know that now.

But, that isn't the reason that I ended up having a bad day.

My day went all wrong when I arrived at school.

I put my bag in my locker and went into our classroom. Mrs. Green wasn't there. Instead there was a lady standing behind Mrs. Green's desk, writing her name in loopy letters on the board. Miss Gray-Smith. I had never seen her before.

I walked to my desk, took out my pens (two blue and two red) and lined them up on my desk, lids pointing to the right, ready for the day. I actually have two desks all to myself. There is my desk and the empty one next to it.

The bell rang and Miss Gray-Smith turned to face the class. She didn't look nearly as old as Mrs. Green and she was wearing a blue headband with a bow on top of her blond hair, which made her look a little bit like Alice in Wonderland.

"Mrs. Green is away sick today," she said to everyone. "So I'm here for the day with you. I thought that instead of doing spelling this morning, it might be fun if we did some science experiments."

The class cheered, but I put up my hand.

"Yes … umm … sorry, what is your name?" Miss Gray-Smith asked, looking at the class list in front of her.

"Felix," I told her. "Felix Twain."

"Yes, Felix?" Miss Gray-Smith said.

I lowered my hand. "On Monday, first thing, we do spelling."

"I know that, Felix, but I can't find where Mrs. Green has left the spelling words for today. So I thought it might be fun to do some science instead. I've brought along some fun experiments to do. You can do your spelling tomorrow when Mrs. Green gets back."

"But on Monday, first thing, we do spelling," I told Miss Gray-Smith again, trying to be patient with her.

It was obvious to me at this point that the teacher was clearly crazy. We don't do science experiments first thing on Monday. We do spelling. S-p-e-l-l-i-n-g. It is right to do spelling at the start of the day. It is definitely not the right thing to do science experiments. The thought of doing something other than spelling gives me a funny feeling in my stomach, like butterflies flapping their wings in there.

"Thank you, Felix," Miss Gray-Smith said, frowning. "I know that is what you usually do, but today we are going to do something different."

"And fun!" added Gerund O'Toole from the back of the room.

Typical. Gerund would do anything to not do any work.

"And fun!" repeated Miss Gray-Smith with a smile.

She reached into a bag sitting beside Mrs. Green's desk and pulled out a bottle half filled with bright-blue, glittery liquid. Several of the girls in the front row let out an appreciative "Oooh" sound. They were so impressed you would think she had just pulled a unicorn out of her bag.

"This is a mixture of hydrogen peroxide, dish soap, blue food coloring, and some glitter."

She set the bottle down on Samira Chen's desk in the middle of the room. The other kids turned around in their seats so they could get a good look at what was going on. The butterflies in my tummy fluttered their wings more frantically.

"We are meant to be doing spelling," I said, louder this time. I picked up my school planner and pointed to the timetable on the back. "See? First thing on Monday is spelling!"

Miss Gray-Smith pulled out a small, clear canister. She held it up to the light so everyone could see that it contained a brown liquid.

"This is yeast mixed with warm water," she said and waved her hand around it, like a lady on a game show holding up a prize for the contestants to admire.

The class leaned forward, hanging on her every word.

"And when we mix the two together," she said, putting a funnel into the top of the bottle with the blue liquid. "We get…. elephant toothpaste!"

She poured the brown yeast liquid into the funnel and it mixed with the blue liquid. Almost immediately, thick, blue foam filled the bottle. Within seconds, it began to pour out of the top of the bottle like a giant tube of toothpaste being squeezed.

The class gasped in surprise and then they began to clap and cheer enthusiastically.

At that point, I felt the blood start to rush into my ears and it beat there like a drum. The butterflies in my stomach felt like they were the size of bats and their wings were churning up my insides. Everything around me began to disappear into a blizzard, like a television screen filled with static. The voices around me sounded like they were miles away. My chest started to feel all tight. My stomach felt like it was filling with lead.

"Stop! That's not right," I shouted at Miss Gray-Smith and covered my ears with my hands. "The timetable says spelling and that is what we have to do."

Nobody listened to me and it was too late. There was so much going on in my head that I felt like I couldn't see anything and so much noise in my ears that my head felt like it was going to explode. I could have been the only person in the room just then and it wouldn't have mattered. I couldn't have

stopped it. I was stuck.

"This is not right, not right, not right, not right!" I shouted, noise pounding in my head and the feelings on my inside bubbling out all over the place.

I was over at Samira's desk before I knew it and I grabbed the bottle, which was still spewing elephant toothpaste out of the top. Then I shook it really hard so that the thick blue foam flew everywhere. Before I really knew what was going on, there was blue foam on the classroom ceiling, blue foam on the carpet and blue foam on everyone in the class.

Every kid in the class was staring at me with looks of horror, while clumps of blue foam clung to their uniforms. Even Miss Gray-Smith, who looked completely shocked at what had just happened, had a large lump of blue foam quivering on the top of her head.

"I told you," I shouted, "first thing every Monday is meant to be spelling!"

Then I ran out of the room.

My head was still full of blizzard as I ran down the hallway as fast as I could, being careful to only step on every second tile to keep myself safe. Right past other classes doing writing, reading, math, spelling or whatever else they are meant to be doing at this time. I'm sure none of them are doing science experiments.

I wasn't clear where I was running to exactly, but then I saw the door to the principal's office was open. Mrs. Lovejoy wasn't in there. It was the perfect hideout. If I closed the door, nobody would know that Mrs. Lovejoy wasn't in there having a private meeting with someone. I could hide in there for hours and nobody would dare to open the door. I ran into Mrs. Lovejoy's office and then, just to be safe, I decided to lock the door.

Once I'd calmed down a bit, I realized that there was a lot that I could do to improve Mrs. Lovejoy's office. To make it better. Safer. So I did.

And now here I am. Sitting in an overstuffed armchair with several damp feathers persistently staying stuck on my school blazer and I am in big trouble with Mrs. Lovejoy. Again.

• • •

Eventually, the door to the office swings open and The Bump walks in, followed closely by the rest of Mom.

Mrs. Troy looks sympathetically at Mom. She presses a button on the intercom to let Mrs. Lovejoy know Mom is here.

Mom looks at me and shakes her head. When people do that, I know that it means that they are disappointed or unhappy with you.

"Mrs. Twain," says Mrs. Lovejoy, appearing at the door of her office. "Please come in."

I watch as Mrs. Lovejoy guides Mom into her office, before brushing a puddle of water off her desk and sitting down primly on her fancy leather chair. I watch Mom look around the office. I've done a good job. It is barely recognizable from when I first started improving it about an hour ago. I follow Mom's gaze to the paired books, the reorganized paintings, the shredded scatter cushion, the feathers and the water. Drips are still plopping from the ceiling and there are sodden feathers covering practically every available surface like very damp snow.

Mrs. Lovejoy folds her hands together and places them on the desk in front of her. Then she sees the pencils that I have stuck into the soil of her fiddlehead fern. Her eyes bulge out of her head a little bit.

Mom takes the blue swimming towel from the lost and found offered to her by Mrs. Troy and drapes it over a chair before gingerly sitting down. As Mrs. Troy clip-clops her way back to her desk, she pulls the office door shut behind her.

Just like before, Mrs. Lovejoy doesn't need to shout for me to hear what she is saying through her paper-thin wooden door. From my position in the armchair, I can hear the conversation quite easily.

"Thank you for coming in so quickly," says Mrs. Lovejoy. "I'm afraid we have been having a few problems with Felix."

"I suspect that this might have something to do with the baby," Mom says. "He isn't exactly pleased about having a new baby brother or sister coming along."

Mrs. Lovejoy nods. "That's understandable. It's going to be a big change for Felix and I can appreciate his anxiety about it. But that doesn't change the fact that Felix's behavior at school has become very disruptive. Well, even more disruptive than it has been in previous years. There have been several serious incidents this year already, even before he knew about the baby. The issue with the guinea pigs, for example."

We used to have five guinea pigs in the school library. I helped one to escape the confines of the cage so that there would be four left. Four is good, just two and two. It wasn't my fault that the escaped guinea pig ran into the art room where Ms. Huckabee was hanging up paintings. Nor was it my fault that she got such a fright that she tripped and fell headfirst into a bucket of blue paint and still looks a little bit like a Smurf.

"There was also the issue with the math textbooks," Mrs. Lovejoy reminds Mom. "Remember? When Felix decided that he would take a permanent marker and black out every question in the book that was an odd number. Now all of Mrs. Murray's textbooks only contain questions numbered 2, 4, 6, 8 and 10. And we cannot ignore the incident with the PE storeroom."

That time, I noticed that there was a lot of sports equipment from the PE shed spread out on the grass near the Year 4 classrooms. I thought it would look better if it were all more clearly organized and tidied away. I spent my break time carrying it all back into the shed and lining it all up in pairs by color, size, and type of equipment. Any piece of equipment that I couldn't pair up had to be thrown into the dumpster behind the staff room. It was tiring work and I had the dumpster nearly full by the end of break time. Mr. Naughton, who teaches PE, who always wears a whistle and who has shorts that are far too short, was not very happy with me. How was I supposed to know that he had intentionally set up the equipment that way for an obstacle course? And is it my fault that he still smells like trash after rescuing all of the equipment from the dumpster?

"Felix's personal rules are becoming a problem. He is quite obsessed with following them and doesn't seem to cope if he can't. They are holding him back from learning at school and now it seems to be getting to a point where it is becoming dangerous to those around him. We just can't have one set of rules for Felix and then a completely different set for the other children. It isn't working."

"We have tried so many things at home, but none of them seem to be getting through to him. It doesn't seem to matter what we say or do, he is so … so … so committed to his rules and his routines," says Mom. She sounds tired. "What can we do about it, Mrs. Lovejoy? Really, what can we do?"

Mrs. Lovejoy pauses for a moment to brush off a wet feather that has become stuck to her jacket pocket.

"Well, at the very least, Felix will need to start seeing the school counselor, Mr. Fielding. I know that you haven't wanted him to see the counselor before now, but things can't keep going this way. If Felix doesn't start to make changes to his behavior, we might have to start looking at other options for him."

"Other options?" Mom asks.

"Put it this way, Mrs. Twain," says Mrs. Lovejoy,

tight-lipped, "if Felix doesn't improve his behavior, you will have to look into other ... educational facilities."

"You mean, other schools? You mean, he'll be expelled?" I can hear the worry in Mom's voice. "Please, Mrs. Lovejoy. Felix needs to finish the year here at Scribbly Gum so he can go to Green Hill. His brother and sister are there already. We need them to accept Felix there too. They'll never take him if he is expelled from primary school and there isn't another middle school around for miles and miles. Where else would he go?"

"All the more reason for him to change," says Mrs. Lovejoy.

Six

We drive home together and the inside of the car is extremely quiet. Mom has told me when people are really upset about something, they sometimes don't say much. I think this might be one of those times.

As we pull into the driveway, I decide that I should say something to make Mom feel better. I don't want her to be unhappy.

"Look, I don't know what Mrs. Lovejoy is talking about," I tell Mom, opening my door and climbing out. "She's being ridiculous. There aren't that many rules that I have to follow."

I tap the car door handle twice before closing it. Mom raises her eyebrows at me as she maneuvers The Bump out from behind the steering wheel and closes the car door.

"I think we might wait until Dad gets home to talk about this, Felix," says Mom. "In the meantime, I think you should get on with your chores."

Nobody likes doing chores, but they have to be done every day or you don't get dessert. That's the family rule. My job for this week is to fold the laundry. Alice's job for the week is to unload the dishwasher. Henry's job is to set the table. Lavender's job for the week is to try not to kill the goldfish. Every week we swap jobs. Doing the goldfish is definitely the hardest job because they die a lot. One day they are swimming along happily, minding their own business, and the next minute they are dropping like flies. Or rather floating on the top of the bowl like flies. We've even stopped giving them names now. They're just called One, Two, Three and Geoffrey, the only fish from our original four fish that we have left. He belongs to Lavender and I think he must secretly be a robot fish to survive this long.

My favorite job is folding the laundry because I like pairing the socks then putting everything away in the best location for it. If my family is lucky, I even tidy up their closets and put all of their clothes away in the right place for them too. Sometimes they don't like it when I do this, especially Alice and Henry. Mom says it is because they like their things organized their own way. This doesn't really make sense. Why wouldn't they want their things organized the right way?

At 6:30 p.m., just as I finish ironing, folding and putting away the last of Henry's Spider-Man underpants, Dad opens the back door and nearly pulls the whole thing clean off its one remaining hinge. He's a renovator, but the only house he hasn't worked on is ours.

Dad used to be a math teacher, which is a very sensible and respectable job. He never used to be a renovator at all. I don't think he even owned a hammer. Then overnight, everything changed.

I blame television. Alice says that we should have been more careful about what we let him watch.

Instead, we thought it would be all right if he watched a few episodes of *Rescue my Renovation* and *Pretty Big Designs* one night.

Big mistake. Suddenly, Dad began to fancy himself as a renovator. He bought all of the tools and the kind of clothes that you need to look like a builder. He did the calculations and worked out how much money he could make by fixing up people's houses for them, just like they do on TV. Then he started spending meal times holding up paint chips and saying things like "Do you prefer the clotted cream, the eggshell, or the off-white paint color?" (even though everyone at the table is thinking that the three cards he is holding up are actually all the same color) and "I really like what that Jeremy Jury did with the outdoor room in that last episode of *Backyard Bitz*" (even though everyone in the family is wondering what on earth an outdoor room is and isn't it just the same as a backyard?).

Then Dad quit his job, sold our perfectly good

house and bought a new place just around the corner. And when I say new place, I don't mean new. New to us, but extremely ancient in every other way. Dad calls it a "fixer-upper," but I think it is more of a "faller-downer" personally.

I didn't want to move. I liked our old place. It was familiar and cozy and really nice, even if I had to share a room with Alice and Lavender. At least they don't smell and groan like they are dying.

We somehow avoided talking about what happened at school for most of dinner. From Henry's grunting, we manage to understand that he made the soccer team at school. Alice says that she didn't know they were accepting apes on the team. She then tells a very long-winded story about two girls at school who got the wrong lunch order, with the girl who wanted the meat pie getting the mac and cheese and the girl who wanted the mac and cheese ending up with the pie. To solve their problem, they apparently ended up combining their lunches to have a mac and cheese pie.

I watch as Lavender sticks some peas in her ears, but nobody else seems to notice. Mom tells us that the baby is currently the size of a butternut squash. I don't know why they measure babies using food. Two weeks ago, the baby was the size of a cauliflower, and by the time it is ready to be born, Mom says that it will be the size of a watermelon. I'd rather have a watermelon than a new brother or sister. Watermelon is delicious and much less stinky.

Dad tells us about a couple he met today who are considering hiring him to be in charge of the renovations for their house. They want their house to look more like a castle and their plans include adding a moat, a drawbridge, and two turrets at the front.

"And how was your day, Felix?" asks Dad, as he finishes the last of his carrots.

"It was fine," I tell him.

"Really, Felix?" says Mom, giving me a look that says that I'm not going to get away with not telling Dad about what actually happened at school today.

"Yes, it was great. And I think I have homework to do," I say, pushing back my chair. "I'd better get started right away!"

I take my plate and cutlery to the dishwasher, grab my schoolbag from beside the door and scamper off down the hallway before we can begin discussing the not-so-good details of my day.

At the end of the hallway, I turn left and pull open the door to reveal the stairs-beneath-the-stairs, which lead to a tiny room underneath our house. Dad says that it probably used to be a cellar, although it wouldn't have been very good as it isn't very cold down there. Only Alice, Lavender and I can stand up comfortably in here. The others are too tall and the girls don't like it because they are afraid of getting stuck down here in the dark. So it has become where I come to hide from the rest of my family when I just want time by myself.

There isn't much stuff in here, as it is a very, very small room. It makes Harry Potter's cupboard under the stairs look very roomy. All I have is a beanbag, a blanket, a light bulb on a string hanging from the roof, and a small table to hold my ark collection.

I began collecting arks when I was born. I didn't exactly know that I was collecting them when I was just a baby, obviously, but as I've grown, so has my ark collection. When I was a little baby, Mom and Dad decided that my name was going to be Noah. They called all of their friends and told them that they had just had a baby boy and that my name was Noah Felix. Then, after about two weeks, Mom decided that it wasn't quite the right name. She said that it made her think of an old man with a long white beard, just like Noah from the Bible. So Mom and Dad decided that I would just be Felix Noah instead. They'd just switch my two names around and it wouldn't be a big deal.

The problem was that by then all of their friends had rushed out and bought baby presents for me. They had all thought they were very clever by giving gifts that were Noah's ark themed. As a result, I now own four different arks – one plastic, one made from stuffed animals, and two wooden ones (one plain wood and one brightly painted).

I have eight different copies of the story of Noah, several framed pictures of his ark and even a quilt for my bed that has two animals for every letter of the alphabet on it, with a big ark at the bottom. It has become my thing now and I still get given Noah's ark themed gifts by some of my relatives for my birthday.

There is a knock on the door at the top of the stairs and it opens a crack. Mom's hand reaches in and puts down a plate with two chocolate cookies. I was in such a hurry to get away from the table that I forgot about the best bit: dessert!

"Thanks," I say, reaching up and taking the cookies.

"Half an hour before bedtime, Felix," says Mom and she closes the door.

I eat my cookies and check that my animals are all in the correct position, lined up two by two in their places inside the ark. I take each of them out and polish them with a cloth that Mom gave me from the cleaning cupboard. Then I put them back in their exactly right spots. Two by two.

There is only one problem with my collection. I have an elephant problem. It is a big, obvious thing to have a problem with. When I was younger and Alice was just a baby, we were playing with one of the arks, the one with the plain wooden animals, on the rug in the family room. Mom was doing some vacuuming around us and was being extra careful not to suck any wooden animals into the vacuum cleaner. In fact, she was watching the nozzle of the vacuum cleaner so carefully that she didn't see the elephant under her foot until it was too late.

We glued it back together and it still stands up OK, but it doesn't look the same as the other one. Mom wanted to throw it away, but I wouldn't let her. Ever since then, I've kept all of my animals safely tucked away in their arks. That way, they will be safe.

When I'm satisfied that all of the animals are clean and have been put away correctly, I turn off the light and climb up the stairs two at a time.

I close the door under the stairs behind me and continue upstairs to bed. Two. Four. Six. Eight. I'm halfway up when Lavender appears at the top in her nightie, almost ready for bed.

"Have you seen Ruggy?" she asks me. Ruggy is Lavender's baby blanket that she still loves even though she is not a baby anymore.

"I don't think so," I tell her. "Where did you put it when you got up this morning?"

Lavender scratches her head. "I think I might have put it in the sink when I went to the bathroom."

"Then it is probably still in the bathroom," I tell her. She runs off, then reappears at the top of the stairs a moment later holding Ruggy. She waves the blanket in the air triumphantly to show me before galloping off around the landing to her bedroom.

It is then that I realize I have lost track of which step I am on. I walk back down to the bottom of the stairs and begin again. Two. Four. Six. Eight. Ten. Twelve. Fourteen. Sixteen. I brush my teeth for two minutes and I'm in bed before Dad even comes around to tell us that it is time for lights-out.

"Good night, Henry," says Dad, reaching down and patting the person-shaped lump in Henry's bed.

The lump grunts something that sounds like good night in reply.

Dad sits down on my bed. He has to duck so that he doesn't bash his head on the top bunk. He's still wearing his paint-spattered overalls and steel-capped boots.

"Mom told me about what happened today at school," he says.

I fiddle with my blankets and pretend not to hear him.

"You can't just go around shouting at teachers and locking yourself in principal's offices, you know, Felix," he continues. "You need to start controlling your temper. You can't just get mad at everyone who doesn't do what you want. People don't like it if you're angry with them all the time."

"There are just some things that have to be done the right way and sometimes other people don't understand how to do them properly," I tell Dad. "I don't like it when things aren't done right. It makes me feel all funny inside."

Dad looks at me thoughtfully. I can tell from the look on his face that he doesn't really get it. Then his eyes begin to wander around the bedroom. His gaze stops on the paint peeling off the walls, the dirty marks on the carpet, and the cupboard doors that have come off their hinges. When he sees all of the things that need fixing, his renovator's brain stops thinking about all of my problems and starts thinking about our house's problems.

"Maybe this weekend we could do up your room a little bit?" he says, thinking out loud. "We could strip the walls and replace the carpet. How would you like to pick the new colors?"

I shake my head. "I don't think so. I don't want it to change. It is OK as it is."

"Maybe we could do the family room then? Maybe I could just fix up the fireplace so we can use it? Or hang some pictures in the hallway?" Dad suggests.

I sit up in bed. "No. You can't change it. It has to stay the same."

"All of it? Can't I just fix up a few things? Small things?"

I shake my head. I'm starting to get that same funny feeling in my stomach, like the one I had today.

"No! You just can't. Please, Dad."

Dad sighs. "OK, we'll leave it just as it is."

"You have to promise," I tell him. "Promise!"

"OK, OK. I promise." Dad holds up his hands in surrender. "Now, good night, Felix," he says, standing up. "It's time to go to sleep."

"Good night, Dad. Good night, Dad," I tell him.

Eight

"So I've found you a time to go and see Mr. Fielding today," says Mom as we pull up at school. "Mrs. Lovejoy thinks that he might be able to help you to look at some of your rules and some of the school rules and see if maybe they could work together."

I make a face at Mom. "I'll go," I tell her, "but he'll just say that you are all being completely silly and that I don't need to see him."

"OK," says Mom, resting her hand on The Bump. "If that's what he says, then you won't have to go and see him anymore."

"Good," I tell her and climb out of the car after the others.

I'm pleased to see that everything has returned to how it should be when I walk into the classroom. For one thing, Mrs. Green is back at school, and apart from some blue stains on the ceiling where the elephant toothpaste splattered, the classroom is looking exactly right. I go to my pair of desks and take out my pens: two blue and two red. Then I sit

at my desk, cross my hands in front of me and wait for class to start.

There are some other students already here. Samira Chen is sitting on her desk chatting to the twins Daisy and Maisie about some boy band that they all really like. Oscar and Gerund are at the back of the room, throwing a scrunched-up ball of paper back and forth. Emma and Alva are sitting huddled together feverishly reading a physics book and there are others playing cards near the door or chatting outside in the hallway.

"Good morning, everyone," says Mrs. Green.

She claps her hands together twice. This gets everyone's attention and they take their seats at their desks. "It is great to see you all. I'm feeling much better, although I've heard that yesterday was such an exciting day that you are probably wishing that I would be away more often."

Several sniggers escape from people's mouths and Gerund O'Toole has such a big grin that you would think it would be hurting his face to smile that much. The twins can't help but let out a little giggle. I can feel a lot of eyes staring at me.

"Now, today we have a –" Mrs. Green stops. The classroom door opens.

There is a girl standing in the doorway. She is wearing the red and blue Scribbly Gum school uniform, but it doesn't look the same as mine. She

has stripy tights on under her shorts and a long-sleeve black T-shirt under her red polo shirt. On her hands are woolly black gloves with the fingers cut off. Her ponytail is long and very red. She is wearing a black headband with tiny cat ears on it and a belt around her waist that has a long black tail attached to it.

"Perfect timing," says Mrs. Green. "Today we have a new student joining us." She waves at the girl, gesturing for her to come into the room. The girl takes a step forward.

"This is Charlottina Pye," announces Mrs. Green. "She is new to Scribbly Gum Primary School. I hope you will all make her feel welcome."

She smiles at the girl.

"Why don't you tell us a bit about yourself? Like where have you been at school before here, Charlottina," she says.

Charlottina Pye looks at Mrs. Green. "Actually, nobody calls me Charlottina. It is a long and completely ridiculous name. My mother made it up. I'm actually just Charlie. And I've been to Red Hill Primary, Davison Street Primary, St. Magdalene's School for Girls, Murphy and Winkleton District Primary School, and Smith House School."

"Wow, that's quite a few schools in your lifetime, Charlie!" says Mrs. Green, surprised.

"That's just the schools I've been to this year," says Charlie and shrugs.

"That's… well, that's… a lot." Mrs. Green doesn't quite know what to say. This is a rare occurrence.

Finally, she finds her voice. "OK then. Why don't you go and sit next to..."

She pauses and looks around the room. Her eyes stop at the empty space next to mine. They keep going, scanning the rows of tables, then come back to rest on the spare desk next to me once more.

"Next to Felix," she finishes and points to where I am sitting.

The class all watch as Charlie walks down the aisle and slips into the seat next to mine. It feels like they are all holding their breath, waiting for something to happen. I don't mind if she sits at the spare desk next to me. Nobody sits there at the moment because when Mrs. Green gives everyone the chance to choose where to sit, nobody chooses to sit next to me.

"Right," says Mrs. Green, shuffling some papers, "let's get started with geography."

She hands Alva Banky, our Class Captain, a pile of papers and Alva walks around the room handing them out. Alva is very good at her job.

"Could I please borrow a pen?" Charlie whispers, as Alva puts two world maps down on our table. "I forgot to bring my pencil case."

I look at the pairs of pens lined up on my desk, two blue and two red.

If one runs out, then I have the other to use as a backup. If I give one to Charlie, then I definitely wouldn't have one as a backup anymore. Then, if the one I'm using ran out, I would have nothing to write with. Then I couldn't do my work. Then I wouldn't learn anything. Then I wouldn't be able to move up to Year 6 next year. Then I couldn't go to middle school. Then I couldn't go to university. Then I might not be able to get the job I want. Then I won't have any money. Then I would be homeless.

"No," I hiss back at her. "No way!"

"What?" Charlie whispers back. She looks surprised, like I might have misheard her. "I just want to borrow a pen."

"I said no. I don't have a spare one that I can lend you. OK? Go away."

Charlie looks at the four pens on my desk, then shrugs and turns to Emma sitting at the table on the other side of her. Moments later she turns around holding a blue pen, a red pen and even a sparkly silver glitter pencil with a fancy cat eraser on the end.

On Tuesday morning, we do geography. Mrs. Green knows the timetable and has prepared her lessons accordingly. I appreciate this. We spend the morning labeling our world maps with countries of the world and their capital cities. I'm good at remembering them because they come in twos. Each country has a matching capital city. Perfect pairs.

When the bell goes for break, the whole class spills outside into the playground.

I get a banana out of my bag and head straight for the old gum tree log by the monkey bars. This is my happy spot.

Charlie comes out and sits down on the other end of the log. My log. And starts to eat a carrot. A whole carrot with the skin and all.

I peel my banana and begin to eat. It is hard to concentrate with all of the carrot crunching that is going on.

I glare at Charlie, but she doesn't seem to realize that she is sitting on my log chomping on her carrot.

"Is this what you do every break time?" she asks me. "Do you just sit here by yourself?"

I shake my head. "I only do this at snack time. At lunchtime, I mostly go to the library."

"Do you like to read books then?" Charlie asks.

"No," I tell her. "Not particularly."

I get asked this question a lot. Most people then ask me why I go to the library if I don't like to read, but if Charlie thinks this is odd, she doesn't say anything.

She watches all of the other kids in the school, running around in groups or playing with friends.

"We could play a game here on this old log," she says, finally. Then, using her hands to keep herself steady, she carefully pulls herself up to her feet.

"Like, can you do this?" she says and strikes a pose like a ninja. "Hey-yah! Yah! Yah!" she shouts, moving to a new karate-style pose every time she shouts "Yah!"

"Or we could have a competition to see who can fit more footsteps in as they walk from one end of the log to the other. Ready?"

Charlie shuffles back so she is standing at the very end of the log, adjusts her cat headband and puts her arms straight out to the sides to help her balance. Then she puts one foot directly in front of the other and counts every time she takes a step.

"One, two, three… c'mon, Felix, you have to get up and try. We could race. You could start from one end and I could start from the other end and we could see who gets to the middle the fastest with the smallest steps possible."

I take another bite of my banana.

One of the twins, Daisy (or is it Maisie?), comes over to where we are sitting.

"Want to play with us? Samira, Maisie and I thought we would play a game of 'What's the time, Mr. Wolf?' Want to join in?" she asks.

Charlie smiles and slides down off the log. "That would be nice."

She begins to follow Daisy or Maisie over to the space they have cleared along the side of the sandbox. I take another bite of my banana.

Charlie stops walking and turns back to me. "C'mon, Felix. You can play too."

"Sure, Felix, you can play too," Daisy says.

She bites the edge of her lip. Charlie gestures for me to follow them. I finish the last bite of my banana, fling the peel into the trash can and slide off my log.

I follow the girls over to the edge of the sandbox and we line up in a straight line along the edge. Samira is going to be Mr. Wolf first and stands about sixty feet away with her back to us.

"What's the time, Mr. Wolf?" we chant.

Samira turns around. "Two o'clock," she calls back. We all take two steps forward.

"What's the time, Mr. Wolf?" we chant again.

"It's six o'clock," says Samira and we all step six paces toward her. It is an exciting game because you never know when the wolf is going to shout "Dinner time!" then chase you back to the starting line.

"What's the time, Mr. Wolf?"

"Three o'clock," she says.

We all step toward Samira, but I can't stop on three steps, so I just take two.

"Felix, you need to take one more step," says Maisie. "She said three o'clock."

I shake my head. "I'll just take two."

"You can't just take two," says Daisy. "Otherwise we will end up being closer to Samira and when she says 'Dinner time!' than she will be able to catch us more easily than she will be able to catch you."

"And that isn't fair," adds Maisie.

"Fine," I say and take two more steps forward.

"Now you've taken four steps, Felix," Samira calls out.

"But I don't want to take three," I explain.

Daisy and Maisie look at each other. "But those are the rules of the game, Felix. You can't change the rules as you go along."

"Can't we just play with even numbers?"

Samira sighs and leaves her post to join the conversation. The game has clearly come to a standstill.

"That only gives us six numbers to play with, Felix. We can only use two, four, six, eight, ten and twelve o'clock, which is a bit boring," says Samira.

"Can't we just keep playing the game like normal?" says Maisie.

"Or maybe we could just try it Felix's way and see how it goes?" suggests Charlie.

"Can't we just agree to play by the rules of the game?" Samira crosses her arms.

"We're wasting all of our break time arguing," says Daisy.

As if on cue, the bell rings for the end of break and all of the children begin to stream back toward the school building.

"See?" says Daisy. "Break is over. We have to go in."

"But we didn't even finish one game," complains Maisie.

"Why do you have to be so difficult, Felix?" says Samira as we turn to line up with the rest of the class.

Her words sting. This keeps happening to me. We try to play and I ruin the game. I don't do it on purpose. I don't choose to feel this way. I just don't know how to explain that to them.

• • •

After break, Mrs. Green reminds me that I have my appointment with Mr. Fielding. Even though I've never actually been in there, I know where his room is. It is off a short hallway near the school cafeteria and everyone in the school knows where the school cafeteria is. And even if you didn't know where it is, you could just sniff the air and follow the smell of meat pies all the way there.

I count the number of steps between our classroom and Mr. Fielding's room. It is exactly 66 steps, which is a good number.

When I arrive, I can see down the hallway that the door to his room is already open. There is a man sitting at a desk inside. He is very tall and thin. It is like he is half the width of a normal man, but twice as tall. He has hair that is all shaved very short and he is wearing a shirt and tie.

"Mr. Fielding?" I say when I reach the start of the hallway.

"Felix?" the man says, looking up, and I nod. He gets up from his desk and comes over to meet me. He is wearing shorts, colorful socks and leather shoes with his shirt and tie.

"I'm Hugo Fielding," he says. "You can just call me Hugo if you like."

Hugo holds out his hand to me. This is strange because I have never shaken hands with a teacher before and I have never called a teacher by their first name before either.

"Hello, Hugo. Hello, Hugo," I tell him, as I shake it.

It feels strange. I can't imagine calling Mrs. Green by her first name (which is Olive) or Mrs. Lovejoy by her first name (I don't know what her first name is, but I bet it's something like Maureen, Doreen, Noreen, or Boring).

"Come in," says Hugo, gesturing toward his room.

"Your name is even," I tell him as I follow him in.

Hugo looks at me.

"H-u-g-o-F-i-e-l-d-i-n-g," I tell him, pointing to the sign on his door. "That's 12."

"My middle name is Washington," Hugo says.

"Washington!" I exclaim. "What sort of middle name is that?"

Hugo doesn't answer me. He is busy counting on his fingers. "I think my whole name is 22."

I count in my head. He's right.

"22 is good," I tell him. "Actually, it is very good. It has two in it, which is the best number, and it is also a double number because it is two and two, so that makes it twice as good. It is my favorite."

Hugo smiles and sits down in one of the two armchairs in his room.

It is completely obvious that his room isn't the same as Mrs. Lovejoy's room. Her room has uncomfortable armchairs and piles of boring books. Hugo's room is all soft and comfy. There are some huge beanbags in one corner and a pile of knitted blankets in another. Perhaps the most unusual feature is that his couches are pink, which is something else that is new to me. All of the couches I have sat on before now have been brown or gray. I don't mind the pink couches because they have even numbers of cushions on them, which is the best number to have.

I sit down on one of the couches, between

the two cushions – one that is shaped like a little orange fox and one that is made of sort of bumpy, yellow fabric.

"So, Felix," Hugo begins, "what have you come to see me about?"

"Mrs. Lovejoy told Mom to tell me that she wanted me to come see you," I tell him. "She thinks I'm being difficult. I've come to see you so that you can tell me that they are both being utterly ridiculous and then I won't have to come and see you anymore."

Hugo nods, but doesn't say anything. There is a little pocket of silence floating around in the room and it quickly starts to grow longer and bigger.

"It's nothing personal," I tell him, cutting into the silence before it can grow awkwardly large. "I'm sure you're really nice and it would be OK to come back and see you. It's just that I don't think that we really have anything to talk about."

Hugo smiles. "That's OK. I'm good at finding things to talk about. I know lots of interesting facts. Like did you know that elephants have fantastic memories? And that they are actually afraid of mice?"

"Those are definitely interesting facts," I tell him. "I don't really know any facts to tell you in return though."

Hugo smiles. "That's OK. Maybe next time you come to see me, you could bring some to share? My door is always open and I'm good at talking.

I always have some facts up my sleeve. And I'm also not bad at helping people to solve their problems. And actually, you know what we could talk about? Well, Mrs. Lovejoy mentioned that you had a few problems at school yesterday. We could talk about that if you'd like?"

"Oh, that wasn't actually my fault. Mrs. Green was away and the teacher that came to replace her didn't know that we were meant to be doing spelling. Doing the right thing at the right time is important, you know."

"I know," Hugo says. "But would it have been OK if you had done science instead of spelling?"

"Not really," I tell him.

"But why not?" Hugo asks.

"Because it just isn't the right thing to do."

"But why not?" Hugo asks again.

This makes me feel a bit annoyed. I've already answered his question once already. Maybe he didn't hear me?

"Because it just isn't the right thing to do!" I say each word loudly and slowly to make sure he understands.

"Look, Hugo," I tell him. "The timetable says spelling, so that is what we should be doing first thing on Mondays. OK? OK! I'm not the one that has a problem here. The teacher who can't read the timetable is the one that has a problem!"

And with that, I open the door and charge out

into the corridor. I don't just walk back; I'm feeling so mad that I stamp like an elephant for every single one of the 66 steps back to class.

Back in the classroom, it is English time and everyone is reading and answering questions about what they are reading in their workbooks. If Mrs. Green is surprised to see me back so soon, she doesn't say anything.

Charlie is sitting in her seat, next to mine, and she looks like she is deeply engrossed in the book she is holding. When I sit down, however, it is then obvious to me that Charlie is not reading the book in her hands at all. She has a comic book tucked inside.

"You're not meant to be reading that," I tell her. "You're meant to be reading *Bridge to Terabithia* and answering the questions in your notebook."

"Have you ever read a comic book?" Charlie replies, her eyes never leaving the page.

I shake my head.

"Would you like to?" She slides the comic out from inside her book and holds the comic book out to me. I take it. The pages are dog-eared and so worn that they feel as thin as a spiderweb between my fingers.

The cover says *Superman* in bright-red and blue block letters.

"He's one of my favorite superheroes," whispers

Charlie. "He looks like a normal person, but when he takes off his glasses and he changes into Superman, he can do lots of things that he can't do when he is his normal self."

I flip through the pages and each one is filled with lots of bright boxes filled with characters, scenery and speech bubbles. It actually looks interesting. But, now isn't the right time to be reading it.

"I can't read that now," I tell her. "I have to read *Bridge to Terabithia* and answer the questions on the quiz that we are supposed to be doing."

Charlie shrugs and tucks the comic book back inside her book. "OK," she says. "You're the one who is missing out by sticking to the rules, Felix."

I take out my pairs of pens and line them up on my desk alongside my quiz paper. Then I open my copy of *Bridge to Terabithia*. What does she mean that I'm missing out? I'm not missing out. She's the one who is missing out by doing the wrong thing and reading her comic book in class. Nothing bad will happen if I sit here and do the right thing. That is the safest thing to do.

• • •

When I get home after school, the house is quiet. We actually live very close to school, so it doesn't take long to walk home.

It's Thursday, which is the day that I walk home by myself. On Thursday, Henry is at practice for his gorilla soccer team, Alice will be prancing around at ballet and Lavender will be at her craft class. Hopefully it isn't beadwork again this week. One of the teachers ended up having to take her to the local hospital emergency department last time after she swallowed five beads. Apparently she was trying to line them up to make a pattern in front of her teeth – blue, green, yellow, blue, green, yellow – but then our neighbor Jemima Scattercushion accidently elbowed her and she got a surprise and swallowed them. Mom told the distraught teacher that she wouldn't worry as much if she saw some of the other things that Mom had found stuck in Lavender's nose and ears lately.

I use my key to let myself in. The house is dark and quiet, but I know Mom must be around somewhere because her handbag is on the kitchen counter. I hang my schoolbag on its hook, open the pantry and help myself to a granola bar and a bag of salt and vinegar chips.

Then I head up the stairs two at a time.

Mom is in her bedroom. Her room is dark and she is lying on her bed with The Bump. It looks like The Bump is hogging most of the blanket. I like Thursday afternoons because it is just the two of us. I don't have to worry about Henry groaning,

Alice listening to music too loudly or Lavender getting something stuck somewhere.

"Hello, Mom. Hello, Mom," I say. I climb up next to her.

"Hello, Felix. Hello, Felix," she replies. "How was your day?"

"I think it was OK," I tell her. "I didn't visit Mrs. Lovejoy's office, so that is probably a good thing."

"I think it is going to be some time before you are allowed to visit Mrs. Lovejoy's office again, Felix," says Mom with a quiet laugh to herself.

"We have a new girl in our class. Her name is Charlie. She wore a cat costume with her school uniform. She sits next to me in class, eats carrots and reads comic books," I tell Mom.

She raises her eyebrows. I can't tell if she is surprised about the cat costume, the comic books or the carrot. Or maybe it is the fact that she sits next to me.

"Mrs. Green probably thought it would be a good idea for her to sit next to you because…" Mom peters off, clearly trying to think of a reason why. "Because you'll make her feel very welcome at Scribbly Gum Primary!"

I nod. "I did try. We ended up on the same log at break time and she showed me her comic book after I went to visit Mr. Fielding."

"And how was Mr. Fielding?" Mom asks, trying to sound casual.

"He has pink couches and is very tall," I say.

"And do you think he might be able help you, like Mrs. Lovejoy thinks he can?"

I open the bag of chips and crunch on a few before I answer.

"He does know a lot of facts, which were interesting to hear. But I'm not sure that I'll go back and see him again though."

"Oh," Mom says. She rubs The Bump again. "Why not?"

I crunch on a few more chips. "Well, I don't think he is very good at listening. He asked me the same question a lot of times. He didn't seem to understand."

"Really?" asks Mom, stealing a chip from my bag and crunching it. "Maybe he was just feeling a bit nervous."

"Why would he be nervous? I'm the one that just met him for the first time."

"Well he just met you for the first time too."

I hadn't thought of that. Do adults really get nervous when they meet kids for the first time?

Mom moves about on the bed, trying to get into a more comfortable position. "Maybe you should give him a second chance?"

I scrunch up the chip bag. "Maybe." I guess I could give Hugo, with his crazy ties and patterned socks, just one more chance.

"Quick, Felix, give me your hand." Mom grabs my non-chip-bag-holding hand and puts it onto her belly. "Can you feel the baby kicking?"

I hold my hand very still on her belly, but I can't feel anything.

"Soon there won't be 6 of us. There will be 7 in the Twain Family," Mom says. "And the baby might be a brother. Think of how much fun it will be to have a little brother, Felix."

I shrug. I can't see how it will be fun. Another baby will make things all wrong.

"And if it is a boy, then you'll have two brothers and two sisters," Mom points out. "Two and two."

"That would be OK, I suppose," I tell her. "Make sure it is a boy then."

She laughs and her round belly wiggles and dances around under the blanket.

"I can't make sure that it is a boy, Felix," she says. "There are some things that happen that are simply out of our control."

Ten

Although I am on a one-man mission to stay out of trouble (particularly when Mrs. Lovejoy is around), it is only a matter of time before things get out of hand again. Four days, two hours, and approximately 48 minutes after the elephant toothpaste incident, my resolve gets put to the test.

"Before we start our math lesson, I want to give you back your quiz papers from yesterday. Generally, I was very pleased with how you all did," says Mrs. Green.

She reaches over to her desk, picks up a pile of papers and begins handing them out to students.

When she calls my name, I reach forward and take my paper.

At the top, circled in bright-red pen, there is a number.

17. 17! The number 17 is leaping out of the page at me, pulsing in front of my eyes.

Mrs. Green has finished handing out all of the papers and is talking about some of the questions on the quiz that students found difficult, but I can barely hear a word she is saying.

Instead, my head is filled with the number 17. It is like it is talking right to me.

I'm gonna get you, Felix. Terrible things are going to happen to you because I'm written on your work. A 17, right here in front of you on the page. That is all I can hear through the fog in my mind.

"No!" I jump up out of my chair.

I grab my test paper off the desk and begin to rip it. One piece into two pieces into four pieces. Soon it is in as many tiny pieces as I can possibly tear it into. I find the piece with the 17 written on it and make sure that it is completely gone, torn to shreds.

I hear every student in the class gasp.

Mrs. Green looks alarmed. "Is everything all right, Felix?"

I turn on her. "Why would you do that?" I snarl at Mrs. Green. "Why would you write that number? Say you're sorry. Say sorry!"

"I'm sorry, Felix," says Mrs. Green. She looks confused, like she doesn't know why she is apologizing. "That is the score you got. I can't change that," she explains.

I scoop all of the little pieces of paper into my hands and throw them at Mrs. Green. They spin and dance through the air like a miniature snowstorm. As I watch the pieces twirl down to the ground and settle on the carpet, I begin to feel calmer.

Slowly, the fog begins to disappear. I can no longer hear the angry voice in my head.

Mrs. Green is looking at me warily, like she is unsure of what I might do next.

The other kids are all looking at me like I'm crazy. Cracked. Completely nuts.

Why doesn't this happen to them too? Why am I the only one that seems to be worried about things being just right? Why is it only me? Why am I the only one who seems to be going mad?

I'm starting to feel better now that the 17 is gone. It is like order has been restored to the universe once more.

I don't think Mrs. Lovejoy is going to see it like that when she hears about it and I decide that I don't want to hang around to find out.

Yanking open the classroom door, I run down the hallway. Instead of heading left toward the office, this time I turn right. The doorway at the end releases me out into the playground. The sky is overcast and gray. The clouds are dark and ominous, like they are up to no good, and feeling drops of rain on my face, I know that staying outdoors isn't an option.

I dart around the end of the next building and pull on the first door handle I come to. It opens easily and I expect to find myself in a deserted hallway near the school cafeteria. Instead, I run in through the doorway and come face-to-face with Hugo carrying a hot meat pie in a paper bag.

"Hello, Felix," says Hugo, surprised. He grasps tight to his paper bag and only just avoids dropping his hot pie on my head.

"Hello, Hugo. Hello, Hugo," I say.

The words are out of my mouth before I can stop them. After our last meeting, I definitely never wanted to see Hugo ever again. It is pretty bad luck running into him of all people in an otherwise empty hallway.

Apparently today is not my lucky day. At that very moment, Mrs. Lovejoy also appears in the hallway. It is like she has a built-in special teacher radar that can sense when there is a student doing something they shouldn't be doing.

"Hello, Hugo," says Mrs. Lovejoy. Then she turns to me and her eyes narrow slightly. "What are you doing out of class, Felix?"

I feel panic start to rise up inside me. I really can't get in trouble with Mrs. Lovejoy again. Not again. Not so soon. I'll be expelled for sure.

"I was just …" My brain freezes up. I can't think of anything worthwhile that would make it OK for me to be out of class. There was a fire? Aliens want me to go out onto the field so they can abduct me? A plague of child-eating ladybugs?

"He was actually just coming to see me, weren't you, Felix?" says Hugo.

I stare at Hugo. He nods and smiles at me, encouragingly.

I nod back at him. "Ummm … yes? I mean, yes! Yes, I have an appointment with Hugo and I didn't want to be late, so I was running."

Mrs. Lovejoy looks at Hugo, who is standing there holding his hot meat pie, and he smiles back at her too.

"OK, well off you go then," she sighs.

She was the one who wanted me to go and see Hugo in the first place. She can't very well now tell me that I'm not allowed to go and see him.

Now I have no choice but to follow Hugo to his office.

"Take a seat," he says and I sit down on a pink couch.

Today I'm sitting next to a cushion that is shaped like a donut with chocolate icing and sprinkles. I swing my legs back and forth and every time they get to the back of the swing I touch them on the ground. Swing forward, swing backward. First foot, second foot. Swing, swing, one, two. Swing, swing, one, two.

I watch Hugo carefully slide his pie out of its paper bag and onto a plate. It looks a bit squashed. I suspect he might have accidentally squeezed it to avoid dropping it on me when we ran into one another. It was actually pretty nice of him to save me from getting into more trouble with Mrs. Lovejoy. He takes a knife and fork from his desk and begins to eat.

"Hugo?"

"Mmmm?" Hugo replies with a mouthful of pie.

"Are you going to make me talk about what happened the other day in Mrs. Lovejoy's office now?" I ask him.

Hugo shakes his head. "You don't have to talk about anything you don't want to, Felix," he says and takes another mouthful of pie. "Really."

"Really, really?" I say.

Hugo nods.

We sit there in silence, with Hugo chewing and me swinging my legs back and forth. Swing, swing, one, two.

"Hugo?"

"Mmmm?" Hugo replies with another mouthful of pie.

"You know two? Like the number?"

Hugo swallows and nods. "I think so. Two comes after one and before three, right?"

I smile. "Yes, that's right. Well did you know that it is the only even prime number?"

Hugo counts on his fingers. "One, two, three, four … Oh, wait, four isn't prime because it is 2 x 2. Then six is 3 x 2 and eight is 4 x 2. Every other even number is a multiple of two. You're right, Felix."

"I know," I tell him. "And two is the third number in the Fibonacci sequence."

"What's the Fibonacci sequence?" asks Hugo.

"It is a series of numbers where the previous two numbers add up to give you the third number. So it goes, 1, 1, 2, 3, 5, 8, 13, 21, and so on. And two is the third number because it is 1 + 1. That is another one of the facts that I know."

"That's pretty interesting," says Hugo. "Thanks for telling me those facts, Felix."

"That's OK. I figured that after the other day it was my turn to share some facts with you." Maybe Mom was right. Maybe Hugo does deserve a second chance.

"Did you know that the Ancient Greeks didn't think that zero was a number?" Hugo tells me. "And they weren't even sure that one was a number either."

I swing my legs back and forth and think about this. That is a pretty crazy fact when you think about it. Hugo does seem to know a lot of interesting facts.

"That means that counting would have just started at the number two!" I suddenly realize. "Do you think that means you'd always have to have things in groups of two or more? Two apples, two scoops of ice cream ... two poodles!" I giggle and Hugo smiles.

He begins typing on his computer again. He keeps going for a full minute. He is a very fast typist. I just sit on the couch. Swing, swing, one, two. Swing, swing, o –

"Hey Felix," says Hugo, interrupting my leg-swinging pattern.

"Hang on," I tell him. I haven't finished that last swing. Where was I up to? I decide to do a full set just to be sure. Swing, swing, one, two. When my second foot touches the ground, I look up at Hugo.

"Yes?" I say. "What?"

Hugo looks at my feet for a moment. "What did you just do then?"

I look down at my feet, then up at Hugo, trying to see what he has seen. "When?"

"With your feet swinging. What did you just do when I interrupted you?"

I'm not sure what he means. I take a guess. "I finished the swing?"

"You finished the swing?"

"Yes, because I was halfway through. You can't stop when you are halfway through."

"Really?"

I nod. "Yes, you have to finish the pattern."

"Or what? What if you don't finish the pattern?"

"Something bad will happen," I tell him.

"Bad?" he asks me.

"Yes, if I didn't finish the pattern right then, something bad would happen. If I don't finish a pattern, then I don't feel right. I get this feeling in my stomach and it doesn't go away until I finish it."

"And are there other things that you do that you have to do or patterns that you have to finish?"

I don't have to think about this for very long before a list begins forming in my mind.

"There are a few," I admit. "Like because there was a 17 written on my quiz paper, that might mean that I could get chased by a small but angry dog on my way home. Or if I put a book back in the incorrect place, tonight there might be a huge flood and all of the books will be ruined. Then there would be no more books for anyone. Or like the ceiling might fall in and the whole class would be crushed by all of that plaster and wood. Or a pipe might burst and the room would fill up with water and we would all drown. Or there might be old electrical wiring in the wall that could spark and start a fire and we would all be burned to death. If we just stick to the rules, we will all be safe."

Hugo gets up from his desk and walks over to one of his bookcases.

"So Felix, I've had an idea. You don't have to do it, but I think it might help you if you do. I'm going to give you this notebook," he says, pulling a small red notebook with a blue elephant on the cover from one of the shelves. "And in return, I want you to write down all of your patterns."

"You want me to write them down?" I ask. "All of them?"

Hugo nods. "Every time you think about something that you have to do because of having to finish a pattern or because of a rule, write it

77

down in the book. When you think you have them all written down, come back and see me again. If you want to, of course."

That doesn't seem too hard. Plus he saved me from Mrs. Lovejoy so now I owe him.

I reach out and take the notebook.

"OK," I tell him. "I'll do it."

• • •

After school, I walk through the doors to the school library and I am immediately in my happy place. The library is a place filled with quiet, organization, and order. Just the way I like it.

"Hello, Felix!" exclaims Miss Claudette, breezing out from behind a stack of books.

Miss Claudette is the teacher in charge of the library. She is short and sturdy, with hair and skin the color of chocolate. She wears dangly earrings, colorful kaftans, piles of bracelets and a different pair of glasses to match her outfit every day. When she smiles, her mouth seems to reach from ear to ear.

"Hello, Miss Claudette. Hello, Miss Claudette," I say.

Although her daily matching earrings-glasses-bracelets-outfit combinations are very impressive, my favorite thing about Miss Claudette is that she likes me coming to the library. I would even go so far as to say that I think she looks forward to me helping out. She says that the library is never as organized on days that I don't come in to help her. I never get in trouble in the library.

"I'm so glad you're here," says Miss Claudette. "I missed you yesterday and there are so many books on the cart for you today!"

She has a strong Caribbean accent that gives everything she says a singsong quality.

"That's OK," I tell her.

I pass behind the circulation desk and pull out a cart filled with books, ready to be returned to the shelves.

I push the cart over to the shelves and begin sliding the books back into their places, ready for a reader to find them and take them home. I love that every book has its own place on the shelf, that everything is sorted and ordered just right.

When I'm finished, I run my hands along the spines of all of the books on the shelves, pushing them back slightly so they are all the same distance from the front of the shelf. Perfectly tidy. Finally, I straighten up the pairs of books on the individual wire book holders at the end of the shelves that allow you to see what is on the cover.

I repeat the process with three more carts of books.

Miss Claudette comes over to help me with the last few books to be put away.

"Now Felix, I heard about your adventure in Mrs. Lovejoy's office," says Miss Claudette.

She smiles then waggles a plump finger at me.

"You had better be on your best behavior between now and the end of the year."

She is smiling, but I also know that she is serious. Her bracelets clatter and jangle together as she slides books back onto the shelves. For someone who works in a quiet place, Miss Claudette is very noisy.

"I'm trying," I sigh. "But it is like I want to do one thing and my brain wants to do something else. When things like that happen, it is like I don't get a say. My brain just takes over and won't stop until everything is right again."

Miss Claudette nods and re-shelves a few more books.

"Your brain does some amazing things too, Felix. You are a wizard when it comes to organizing things in the library. If you get expelled, who will help me with all of the books? We need you here, Felix."

I slide the last book onto the shelf, then I check them all one more time to make sure none of them are sitting farther forward or back than others. I double check to make sure that each is in the correct place according to the little stickers on the spines.

There is a voice inside my head that tells me when they are perfect and then I no longer have the feeling that something awful might happen on my way home. One book out of place and who knows what kind of disaster I could be facing.

Twelve

I'm convinced that Charlie Pye was sent to Scribbly Gum Primary School to make my life difficult. It feels like she deliberately goes out of her way to do things that are not right, just to upset me.

She never has a pencil case or any pens to write with and she always wants to use mine. She never has the correct school uniform. Today she is wearing the red and blue Scribbly Gum uniform with zebra-print leggings underneath and black and white ribbons braided into her long, red hair. She only reads comic books and never hands in her homework. These are just some of the rule breaking things that she does.

Right now, most ridiculously of all, she is eating cereal. For lunch. That's not right. Cereal is definitely a breakfast food.

I watch Charlie plunge her hand into her paper bag and pull out another handful of brightly colored breakfast cereal. Piece by piece, she flips the cereal up into the air, then catches it in her mouth with a crunch.

She sees me watching her and holds out the paper bag to me. "Want to try?"

I shake my head.

"Don't you like cereal?" she says.

"Actually I do," I say.

She wiggles the bag under my nose. "Then take some. I'm happy to share."

"I would, but I can't eat cereal at lunchtime."

Charlie raises her eyebrows at me. "Can't or won't?"

When I don't answer, she adds, "Would it actually hurt you to eat cereal at lunchtime?"

I think about this. It probably wouldn't actually hurt me. I'm sure my body can handle eating cereal at any time of day. Maybe I could try some? I reach my hand out toward the paper bag.

Except that is the wrong thing to do, says a voice in my head. *Think about all of the bad things that could happen if you don't follow the rules.* I pull my hand back from the bag.

"I'd better not," I tell her.

"Suit yourself," says Charlie and she runs off down the hallway and out into the afternoon sunshine.

I call after her. "No running in the hallway either!"

She doesn't seem to hear me, or if she does, she completely ignores me. This is another thing that I find frustrating about Charlie Pye. She seems to have selective hearing, only hearing what she wants to hear.

I follow her out onto the playground and sit on my old piece of gum tree. Charlie swings up onto the monkey bars and hangs there, upside down by her knees. I'm glad she isn't trying to play a game with me again because I still have to write down a few things in my red elephant notebook before I have to go and see Hugo. I'm on my fifth page in the notebook. I didn't realize that there would be quite so many things for me to write about.

When the bell goes, I hop off the log, take my notebook and make a beeline for Hugo's office. I've been slowly growing to like Hugo, over the past few weeks. He always says hello to me in the hallways at school when he sees me. Plus he knows an extraordinary number of interesting facts about so many different things.

"Hello, Felix," Hugo says when he sees me. He stands up from his desk where he has been working at his computer. "You came back. Nice to see you."

"Hello, Hugo. Hello, Hugo," I say.

Hugo sits down on one of his pink couches and I join him, sitting between a green cushion with multicolored pom-poms attached to the front and one that is shaped like a poodle. I hold out the elephant notebook to Hugo, but he shakes his head.

"It's your notebook. Why don't you read me what you have written so far?"

I open the notebook to the first page and begin to read:

"1. When I wake up in the morning, the first thing I must do is to count the slats under the bed.

2. When I get out of bed, my feet mustn't touch the ground at the same time – one foot, then two feet. This rule also applies when standing up from any chair or couch.

3. When I eat breakfast, it must be at my particular spot at the counter.

4. When I open or close the car door, I must tap the handle twice.

5. When I walk up the stairs, I must only touch every second step.

6. When I get to the bottom of a set of stairs, I must jump twice on the spot.

7. When I see someone I know, I always say hello twice.

8. When I'm in class, I must have two of each pen available in case something happens to one of them.

9. When tapping my hands or swinging my legs, I must finish a full set of the pattern in my head. If I lose my spot, I have to begin again from the start.

10. When I see an even number it is good, and an odd num –"

Hugo holds up his hand to stop me. "How many items are there on your list, Felix?"

I flip through the notebook to find the last note that I wrote down.

"Fifty-two," I tell him. "But I'm not sure that I have thought of all of them."

Seeing it all on paper in front of me actually surprises me. I didn't realize that I have quite so many rules. Suddenly, it looks like a very long list.

Hugo nods. He doesn't seem surprised by my list at all.

"Do you think these are things that need to change, Felix?"

I think for a moment.

"They do take up quite a bit of time," I say, finally.

Hugo nods, but doesn't say anything. A long pause begins to fill the space between us.

"And not everyone else likes them," I say, trying to fill the gap and trying to stop the pause from growing any bigger. "They think that I'm being bossy or that I'm trying to annoy them by having to do all of these things. But I'm just doing them because I have to. It means that I don't have many friends."

I look down at Hugo's socks. Today they are covered in black-and-white patches like a Friesian cow.

"Or any friends," I say. "More like, I don't really have any friends."

"If you could, would you change that?"

I continue to study Hugo's socks, sticking out above his brown leather shoes. Part of me likes being on my own. I'm like an island, out there in the ocean, all alone. That means I can do things my own way. How I like them. The right way.

But it is also pretty lonely out there, all by myself.

I don't think I'd like to be by myself forever, even if sometimes it would be easier for me.

So I find myself nodding at Hugo.

"I think having some friends would be OK. It would be good, I think. Well, better."

Hugo gets up and walks over to his desk.

"Take a look at this, Felix," he says.

He turns the computer screen slightly so that I can see it from where I am sitting on the pink couch. It is a picture of a brain.

"Now, this part here is your prefrontal cortex," he says. "That's the part of your brain that is just above your eyes. And see that part in the middle there?"

Hugo points to a section of the brain on the screen that is highlighted in green.

"That's called the basal ganglia."

"The basil what?" I ask. The part of the brain that he is pointing to is sort of curled around itself, like a seed that has just sprouted and is now looking for the right direction to grow up toward the sunlight.

Hugo chuckles. "The basal ganglia. That is probably the part of your brain that is causing you difficulties. It is the part that is involved in making you feel anxious when things don't go exactly right or when things aren't how you might want them to be."

"That green, curly plant bit of my brain does that?"

I lean closer to the screen, trying to get a better look.

Hugo nods. "Yes, when it isn't functioning properly. Scientists think that part of the brain is connected with some of the problems you're having. It is like a bully in your head, telling you what to do all the time."

"So the basil is like a bully inside my head?"

I want to make sure I have things clear.

"Exactly right," says Hugo. "Basil the bully. But together we can fight him."

"We can fight the Basil?"

"Yes. It won't be easy, Felix." Hugo looks serious. "Fighting a bully like Basil is hard. But I think you can do it, if you let me help you. Your mom and dad can help you too, as well as your brother and sisters."

"Even Lavender?"

"Yes, even Lavender. When she isn't busy sticking things up her nose, I'm sure she will be able to help you too, Felix."

"But, how? How do we begin the fight against Basil?"

"OK, Felix. I want you to come into my room and say hello to me."

"Right now?"

Hugo nods. I slide off the couch and go out through the door, pulling it closed behind me.

Then I turn around, knock on the door and go back into the room, just like I'm arriving for the first time.

"Hello, Hugo. Hello, Hugo," I say.

"Hello, Felix," says Hugo. "Now I want you to do it again, but this time you're only allowed to say hello once, not twice."

I sigh and turn around, then come back in through the doorway again.

"Hello, Hugo," I say. But there is a little voice in my head that doesn't want me to stop there. *Say hello again, Felix*, the voice says. *Come on, Felix, just say hello again. If you don't say hello again, Felix, something bad will definitely happen.*

"Hello, Hugo," I add and I'm immediately filled with a sense of relief. Then disappointment.

Hugo shakes his head.

"No, once only, Felix, not twice. That second hello is coming from Basil. He's making you want to say hello twice. You need to tell him that it is OK to just say hello once. You need to tell him that nothing bad will happen if you only say hello once. Repeat after me: Hello, Hugo."

"Hello, Hugo," I say.

Say it again, says Basil in my head.

"Hello, Hugo," I repeat.

Hugo shakes his head.

"You have to say no to Basil, Felix. Stand up to him. He's a bully. This time, I want you to try to count to ten before you add anything. "

"Hello, Hugo," I say. 1, 2, 3, 4 ...

Say it again, says Basil in my head. I shake my head. 5, 6 ...

Come on, Felix, says Basil. *Say it, say it, say it*. I clamp my teeth closed and refuse to say it. S*omething bad will happen to you,* nags Basil. *Something bad. Something awful.* 7, 8, 9, 10. I finish counting as quickly as I can. It is hard to think because my head is so full of Basil.

"Hello, Hugo," I say, for the second time.

I feel Basil relax almost immediately.

"Let's do it again," says Hugo. "This time you need to try to do it while I count to twenty. Ready?"

I nod. "Hello, Hugo."

The moment I say it Hugo starts counting.

I sit still and try to concentrate on not adding a second greeting. Basil is right there, trying to bully me into saying it again.

Be quiet, Basil. I shout at him in my head. *Be quiet, be quiet, be quiet*. I can feel Basil getting mad. I start getting that funny feeling in my stomach. I close my eyes and put my head in my hands. I wait for everything to go wrong, but nothing happens.

"Twenty!" says Hugo. "Well done, Felix! Well done!"

Nothing bad happens at all.

When I finally open my eyes, Hugo is smiling. He puts his hand out and gives me a massive high five.

"Let's try it again. Hello, Felix."

"Hello, Hugo," I say.

Basil is still there and he is mad about before. *Say it, say it, say it*, he says to my brain. My stomach still feels funny and I have a strange feeling behind my eyes, like my heart is beating in my head. It is hard work, but I manage to keep the second "Hello, Hugo" from coming out. It feels like I have a mouthful of Brussels sprouts; I want to spit them out, instead I'm being forced to swallow them.

"You're doing great, Felix. Just think of it as a bit like going to the gym," says Hugo. "When you first start going, every muscle hurts and every weight that you pick up feels like it weighs a ton. Over time, it gets easier because your muscles get stronger. It's the same with your brain. The more you work at this, the stronger your brain will get at

standing up to Basil. One day, you could even be able to do it without even thinking about it."

I can't imagine it being easier. I can't imagine my brain not being filled up by Basil, taking up all of my thoughts, bossing me around and making me crazy.

"So, your homework for tonight and for the weekend is to keep practicing, OK?" says Hugo, standing up and showing me to the door. "Remember, it isn't going to be easy or perfect, but it is definitely going to be worth it."

Fourteen

When I get home, everyone is already there. Alice is prancing around the family room dancing to music that only she can hear through her headphones. Lavender is sitting in the craft corner scratching her nose and looking at a jar of tiny, sparkly pom-poms, which she has emptied onto the table. I can't see Henry anywhere, but judging by the muddy sports shoes and the socks that smell like they haven't been washed in three years, he must be grunting away somewhere in the house. Mom is sitting on the couch with a cup of tea resting on The Bump and Dad is standing by the wall in the family room.

I say hello to everyone in turn, starting with Lavender and working my way up from youngest to oldest. By doing it quickly, I manage to avoid saying hello twice, but when I get to Dad I'm thrown off track by the fact that he looks very guilty. When I look closer it is obvious that he is hiding something behind his back and I forget all about the fact I'm meant to be practicing not saying hello twice.

"Hello, Dad, Hello, Dad," I say. "What are you doing?"

Realizing he has been caught, Dad brings his hands around in front of him to reveal a large paint can and brush in a shade of gray that is apparently called "Swift Greyhound." The cans of paint he brings home always have the weirdest names, like Swiss cheese yellow, hamster brown, mint-to-be green.

"Your mother and I were just talking about what color we might like to paint the family room walls," he says. "Of course, not straightaway, but maybe one day we could …" he adds, looking at me hopefully.

"But not today," I tell him. "Or any time soon. In fact, I think the walls are fine as they are, actually."

Dad looks wistfully up at the wall in front of him. There are several holes in it that I know he desperately wants to fill in, as well as picture hooks in odd places and a number of dirty marks that look like they might have come from someone bouncing a muddy basketball against the wall.

The thought of having our family room look different fills me with worries. I like everything to stay the same. I need everything to stay the same. That is the best way to keep everyone safe.

I take my school bag down to my room under the stairs and pull out the math questions I have for homework. They are multiplying fractions questions, just like the ones that we did in class today with Mrs. Green.

I look at the first question: ½ x ¼.

I follow the steps that Mrs. Green taught us; multiply the top line then multiply the bottom line. I end up with the answer ⅛. I do the question twice and end up with the same answer. It can't be right. An eighth is smaller than a half and a quarter. How can multiplying those two fractions together create a smaller number rather than a larger number?

That doesn't make any sense, says the voice in my head. *Multiplication is meant to make numbers larger not smaller.*

"I know," I say to the voice. "Mrs. Green must have it wrong."

I throw my pencil down on my desk in frustration. This is ridiculous. Everyone knows that multiplication makes things bigger.

It is stupid homework, says the voice. *You shouldn't do it.*

Then I realize that I know that voice. It's Basil.

Of course, Basil wants me to quit. He wants me to have a big meltdown about this. He doesn't like changing and he doesn't like learning anything new or different.

I try to picture what Hugo would tell me to do. I imagine that I am in Hugo's office, sitting on his crazy pink couch with its unusual assortment of cushions. He would tell me to stand up to Basil and to say no to him. I'll try that.

"No, Basil," I say.

I pick up my pencil again to show him that I mean business.

I look at the next question: $1/3$ x $1/4$. I do exactly as Mrs. Green taught us and I end up with $1/12$.

See, it's still wrong, says Basil. *You don't understand how to do it.*

I sigh and run my hands through my hair.

"Stop it," I tell Basil.

I scribble out my work for the question and try it again. I still end up with $1/12$.

You might as well quit now. I bet everyone else understands it. They're all going to move on to middle school and you are going to be left behind at Scribbly Gum Primary because you can't get the hang of this simple math.

My head is so full of Basil now that I can't think about anything else. I throw my pencil down on the desk. It bounces several times, then rolls off onto the floor. My head is hurting from the effort of trying to fight back against Basil. I can't think about anything else and I know that he has won.

It's no use. I scrunch up my math questions, shove them back into my bag, then turn my attention to my ark collection.

From the moment I turn my attention away from the math questions and over to straightening up the animals, pair by pair, I feel myself beginning to relax. I make sure each ark's individual animal is lined up parallel to the others, and do the same with each of my framed ark-themed artworks. I take my cloth and dust each animal gently before carefully standing them in exactly the right position alongside their partner.

I leave the wooden elephants until last. I dust the good one first, then I look at the one with the damaged leg. The blue wood is worn and there are several places where the blue paint is chipped away, leaving plain wood exposed underneath. I prop them up next to each other inside their ark, the damaged one leaning against the other one to help it stand, and together they are a complete pair. They need each other, those two elephants.

At break time the next day, Charlie is already waiting for me on the log. Today she is dressed like a poodle. Her red hair is all fluffed up like a fiery halo around her head. There is dark fur trim around her wrists and ankles, and a long brown tail with a large pom-pom on the end.

She is halfway through eating a shiny red apple, which is a surprisingly normal snack for her.

When I don't sit down, she jumps off the log and chases after me.

"Hey! Where are we going?" she asks, catching up.

"I'm going to the library."

She stops walking alongside me.

"Really, Felix? Are you sure? I mean isn't it nicer out here? We could just sit on the log. I won't even make you play a game or anything."

I turn to look at her. "I definitely have to go to the library."

"But you don't even really like books that much," Charlie continues.

"True, but I like going to the library. And I said I would drop by and help out Miss Claudette."

I take a deep breath. "You can come with me if you like. You could help."

I've never invited anyone to join me in the library before and I'm fully expecting Charlie to say no.

Instead, she frowns and reluctantly begins walking alongside me again, crunching her apple as we go and eventually flicking the core into a nearby trash can.

When we get to the library, I hold open the door and usher Charlie inside. There are no other students allowed in here during break time, so we have the place to ourselves.

As I walk around behind the circulation desk and pull out one of the carts filled with books to be returned to the shelves, Miss Claudette pops her head out from her office.

"Great to see you, Felix," she says, her armfuls of bright-orange and green bracelets jangling furiously on her plump arms. "And I see you've brought a friend with you."

A friend? Is Charlie my friend?

"Miss Claudette – This is Charlie Pye. She's new to Year 6."

Miss Claudette's eyes slide over the poodle accessories Charlie has added to her school uniform, but doesn't say anything.

"Nice to meet you, Charlie. Are you going to help Felix? He's our best library monitor. He'll be able to show you what to do."

I push the cart over to the nonfiction section, then begin picking up books and sliding them into their correct location on the shelves. My hands move back and forth over the spines of the books, back and forth, like fingers dance on the keys of a piano. I'm so caught up in what I'm doing that it takes me several minutes to realize that Charlie is just standing there watching me.

"You can put some away too, if you like," I tell her.

She shakes her head.

"It's really easy," I say. "You just look at the numbers on the spine and then put the book in numerical order on the shelf. Like this one," I say, picking up the next book in the pile. "See, this has the spine label 616.85, so you find the 600 section, then you look for the 616 books and once you've found them, then you look at the decimal part and put the book in."

I slide the book into its place on the shelf.

Charlie shakes her head again. "Maybe I can just pass you the books? Then you can put them away in the right place. I couldn't … you're pretty fast at it."

Charlie picks up a book from the cart and hands it to me. I check the spine label and slide it into the correct place on the shelf.

"And this is what you do for fun?" she asks as I work.

I nod and keep working away until finally the cart is empty.

"I find it relaxing. It is easy for me to get lost in the rhythm of putting the books away, each into their correct place. And it makes me feel good knowing that they are all away in their proper place."

I run my hands along the front of the shelves and even out all of the books, making sure they are all sitting exactly next to one another on the shelf. Perfect.

"Maybe you can come back with me another day and help again? I'm sure Miss Claudette wouldn't mind," I say as the bell goes to signal the end of break time.

Charlie shakes her head. "I don't think I'm much help in here, Felix."

"You'll get the hang of it," I tell her. "Even passing the books to me today made the process faster. It was helpful. You'll be putting books away by yourself before you know it. You just have to get used to the system because it is very important for everyone that the books are put back in exactly the right location."

"It's not that. I understand how the system is supposed to work."

"Then what's stopping you?"

For the first time since I've known her, Charlie looks uncomfortable. Her cheeks are red and she seems to be looking everywhere except at me. She mumbles something under her breath.

"What?" I ask.

"Felix. I can't help you in the library because… well, because…"

"What?" I ask again.

"If I tell you, you have to promise not to tell," she says. "It's a very big secret and I don't want everyone to know."

I'm getting impatient now. "Sure, OK. I promise. What?"

"I can't read."

Sixteen

By the time I go and see Hugo on Friday morning, I think I have become a bit stronger at standing up to Basil when it comes to saying hello twice. It is so hard not to say it a second time because Basil is always there reminding me how important it is for me to do it in order to stay safe. While I'm not strong enough to do it every time, I usually hold him off while I count to at least twenty.

There was one time when I accidentally said it twice without thinking, but that was because Lavender popped out from behind a door and startled me into saying it before I even knew what I was doing. The problem with only saying hello once is that it makes me feel very anxious. I'm worried that because I'm only saying it once, something awful is going to happen to me. It isn't a good feeling.

"Hello, Hugo," I say, as I open the door to his room.

Hugo looks up and counts to twenty. When I don't add a second hello, he gives me a thumbs-up.

Hugo is sitting on one of his pink couches reading the newspaper. In his usual shirt, tie, shorts, ankle socks, and lace-up shoes, his long legs look really long and gangly. He looks up at me and smiles, knowing how much I desperately wanted to say it twice.

"Hello, Felix," he says. "Did you know that it is going to be twenty-three degrees Celsius in Melbourne tomorrow?"

Twenty-three. Why would he say that? Twenty-three. Twenty-three!

"And nineteen degrees in Adelaide. It wouldn't be a good day for the beach there."

Hugo shows me the newspaper. He is at the weather section.

Twenty-three. Nineteen. I can feel Basil beginning to get anxious. All of these odd numbers aren't good. *Something awful is going to happen unless you sort this out*, says Basil.

My hand reaches out for the newspaper and I attempt to snatch it out of Hugo's hands.

"Bad luck, Felix," he says, swiftly moving it out of arm's reach. "Ripping up the newspaper isn't an option. You'll have to tell Basil that he will have to be OK with all of these odd numbers. Look, here's another one. Eleven degrees in Hobart. That's practically a summer's day down there."

I grit my teeth and cross my arms. Basil's voice begins to fill my head with bad thoughts. Odd numbers mean that something bad will happen. Like I'll get lost on the way home from school and nobody will ever find me. All of my shoes will disappear. I'll get home and all of my family will have moved without me. The cute, fluffy dog who lives next door will run out onto the road and cause a traffic accident.

"*Stop it!*" I tell him. "*Stop saying those numbers.*"

That's right, Felix, says Basil. *You tell him it isn't OK.*

"Twenty-three, nineteen, and eleven. Twenty-three, nineteen, and eleven," Hugo says.

Then he stops for a second, looks right at me, and adds, "And don't forget about seventeen, fifteen, forty-seven, thirty-one!"

"Stop! Stop it!" I'm shouting now.

Basil is cheering me on. There is no room for any other thoughts in my head apart from what Basil is saying.

"Stop! Stop! Stop! Stop! Stop!"

The words are like lava from a volcano pouring out of my mouth.

"Twenty-three, nineteen, and eleven," Hugo says again. "Eighty-nine, and three hundred and one!"

I can feel my eyes filling with tears. I grab a cushion off his couch and throw it onto the floor. When he doesn't react, I take my foot and stamp on the cushion as hard as I can.

"Say you're sorry," I say. I can feel my eyes filling with tears. "Please, just take it all back."

"I can't," says Hugo.

I take two more cushions off the couch and throw them across the room. One lands on Hugo's desk and the other, shaped like a pineapple, flies out an open window and lands in a rose bush.

"Say you're sorry," I shout at Hugo again.

My face is red and tearstained now.

"We can't give in to Basil in this room," says Hugo simply, as I pummel a cushion with my fists and Basil cheers me on in my head. "You have to win, Felix.

"Take a breath and then take control of Basil. You can do it. You can definitely stand up to Basil about this. But you have to do it. Me saying sorry won't help the problem and it won't fix anything. It will only make it worse. You have to say it and you have to believe it."

I'm so angry that I kick the arm of the couch with my right foot and the impact of it crunches my toes into the end of my school shoes. I grab my foot and hop around for a moment before dropping back onto the couch. I'm momentarily distracted by the pain in my foot and it gives me a second to pause. I draw a breath.

"And another deep breath, Felix," says Hugo, quietly.

My heart's still racing and my head is still completely filled with Basil. When he is really angry he is almost like a dark cloud that gets bigger and bigger, filling my head so I can't see or think properly.

Finally, I manage to calm down enough to speak.

"Please don't say odd numbers, Hugo. I don't like it."

"You mean, Basil doesn't like it," Hugo corrects me. "Why do those numbers upset Basil so much, Felix?"

I explain to Hugo about today's worries, the ones about getting lost on the way home, about the shoes, about my family moving, about the dog and the traffic accident.

"Any of those things could actually happen," says Hugo. "They're unlikely events. Not impossible, but unlikely."

"I don't want them to happen," I say. "That's why I do all of these things. I keep myself safe. To keep everyone safe."

"But avoiding odd numbers won't stop the bad things from happening. Saying hello twice won't stop bad things from happening."

"It has worked so far," I say.

"Has it?" says Hugo. "Has it really? Have all of your routines, rituals, and rules really prevented those things from happening, or have they just not happened on their own?"

This throws me for a second. The logical part of my brain wants to agree with him. *But what if those things are what is actually keeping you safe? What if it isn't just luck?* asks Basil. *How do you know for sure?*

"Isn't it better to do them just in case?" I say. "That way, I'm covered either way."

Hugo shrugs. "The problem with all of your routines, rituals and rules is that you are so busy doing them that you're actually missing out on other things. Your fears and worries? They're holding you back, Felix. Think back to the elephant toothpaste incident. You were so worried about doing something different that you ended up spending the morning in Mrs. Lovejoy's office instead of in the classroom learning."

I furrow my brow. I actually think he might have a point.

"But can I really stop doing all of those things?"

Hugo nods. "I think so, but you're going to have to keep practicing standing up to Basil. A lot. Let's start now. We can take turns at saying odd numbers to each other. I'm going to pick …" Hugo thinks for a moment. "Three. That's mine. Now your turn."

• • •

I'm in Hugo's office for nearly an hour. By the end of the session, I'm exhausted from the mental effort of trying to win over Basil time after time. My cheeks are red and my eyes are feeling scratchy from all of the tears.

As I get back to the classroom, the school bell rings. It is the end of the day and everyone is packing up ready to go home; the room is filled with the sound of chairs being stacked on top of desks and bags being zipped up. I take my two blue pens and two red pens and carefully return them to my pencil box, facing the correct direction.

"So do you want to come over to my house tomorrow?" asks Charlie.

I stop packing up and look around behind me, in case she's talking to someone else.

"Felix, do you want to come over to my house tomorrow?" she asks again.

I haven't been asked to visit someone's house since I went to Lewis' birthday party back in Year 1. There was ice cream, party snacks and so many games to play. They even had a small inflatable swimming pool that was filled with hundreds of brightly colored plastic balls instead of water. I spent ages organizing those balls into color-coordinated piles, then got really upset when the other children wanted to mix them up in the ball pit and play with them. Mom had to come and pick me up early from the party because I was so upset that I started throwing cupcakes at anyone who got too close to the ball pit.

I guess word must have spread around fast because I haven't been invited to any more parties or over to anyone's houses to play since then. And I know it isn't because there haven't been any more parties. The other kids in my class are always talking at school about the fun they have had on the weekend at sleepovers, or going ice-skating, or seeing movies together.

"Are you sure?" I say and she nods. "Do you have a ball pit at your house?"

I need to know what I'm dealing with here.

"Yes, I'm definitely sure, and, no, there aren't any ball pits," Charlie says with a laugh.

"Let me just check to make sure I haven't got something else on," I say, slinging my schoolbag onto my back as we walk out of the classroom and down the hallway.

I pretend like I'm checking through an imaginary calendar in my head to make sure I have nothing else on. I already know the answer.

"Yes, I'm definitely free," I say.

"Great. Write down your address and I'll pick you up at two."

When I clamber into the car two minutes later, I can hardly contain my excitement. Even though I'm tired from my time with Hugo and my cheeks are still tight from the tears, my feet are skipping over the ground and I can't stop grinning. Mom, The Bump and Lavender are already in the car. The Bump is nearly big enough to touch the steering wheel and Lavender is busy with a box of raisins.

As Mom starts the car, I tell her about going to Charlie's place tomorrow.

"That's amazing, Felix," she says. "It will be great for you to spend time with a friend over the weekend."

There is that word again. A friend. The more people say it, the more I am starting to believe it.

"And how are your sessions going with Hugo?" Mom asks as we drive out of the parking lot.

"They're OK," I say. "He hurts my feelings a lot."

"Really?" says Mom.

I nod. "Yes, he makes me do things that are really difficult, and when he does something that makes me feel upset, he never even says sorry."

Mom turns the car onto the road where Alice and Henry's school is.

"But do you think he is helping you?" she asks.

I think about this for a moment. "I actually think maybe he is."

Eighteen

The next morning I'm ready and waiting by the front door at 10:30 a.m., just in case Charlie comes early.

Alice has kindly lent me a giraffe headband that she had when she was in a production of *The Lion King* and I'm wearing some casual clothes picked out by Lavender who said that I definitely should not wear my school uniform to someone's house on the weekend.

Just after the clock in our hallway chimes two o'clock, Charlie arrives at our front gate. She is dressed like a monkey, with little brown ears and a long curly tail. She is riding a bright-red tricycle, but not the small, plastic kind that little kids ride. Her tricycle is the size of a regular bike, with three wheels, two seats (one so that someone can pedal and steer using the handlebars and one alongside, like a sidecar on a motorcycle) and a big basket on the front covered in fancy plastic flowers.

"Nice outfit," she says and hands me a helmet. I carefully put it on and climb into the sidecar.

"See you later, Felix," says Mom and she gives me a wave.

If Mom is a bit surprised by Charlie's mode of transportation, she doesn't say anything. I think that she is so pleased that I'm going to someone's house that even if Charlie had turned up with a beard, twelve earrings, tattoos all over every inch of her body, and riding a purple unicorn, Mom still would have sent me off with a wave and told me to have a great time.

Charlie pushes her bike along the sidewalk, down the driveway and we set off. It is a perfect day. The sun is shining and there isn't a cloud in the sky. Charlie turns the bike out of our street and onto the next one and pretty soon we have enough speed to feel a warm breeze on our faces. It only takes us about ten minutes to get down to the river and we ride along the bike path watching the sunlight glitter on the surface of the water while kookaburras laugh in the trees.

"And we're here," says Charlie.

She pulls on the brakes and her bike comes to a stop. I look around and can't see a single house. Charlie climbs off and I follow her, confused. She pushes her bike up close to the metal railing alongside the path and locks it up. Then she steps from the riverbank across onto the deck of a houseboat parked on the edge of the river.

I stop and stare.

"That's not a house," I tell her.

You're meant to be going to her house, says Basil, getting fired up. *This is not right. Not right!*

"Did I ever say anything about a house?" she says. "I asked you if you wanted to come over to my place. I never said anything about a house."

I think about it for a moment, trying to recall our conversation from yesterday, but I'm forced to admit that she's right.

Stop it, Basil, I tell him, fiercely. *It is a house. It is just a house that floats. That's all. It will be fine.*

I stand still for a moment and count to twenty in my head, calming myself down.

"Come on," says Charlie, unaware of the argument I'm having with Basil inside my head.

She walks down some steps at the front of the boat, opens the front door and lets herself inside.

Rather than stand there by myself on the bank, I take a deep breath and step across onto the boat. *You can do it, Felix*, I tell myself. *It isn't a house, but it is still a home.*

The boat itself is about forty-five-feet long and is decorated with navy and white paint. There are pots of brightly colored flowers on each of the window ledges and what looks like a herb garden on the roof of the boat. There is a scruffy black-and-white dog asleep on the deck and a large blackboard on the railing of the boat says "Pye's Pies & Cakes – Humbly the best in town!" in swirling handwriting and there is a phone number underneath.

I have never been on a houseboat before. I step past the sleeping dog, climb down the stairs and through the door into the cabin.

I'm surprised to see that the inside of the boat looks a lot like the inside of our house. It's just thinner. It's like a family room that has been squashed into a hallway. There is a couch, armchairs, lots of books, cushions, and carpet, just like every other family room I've ever been in. The television is turned on and there is a large, pale boy sitting on the couch. He doesn't look up when I walk in, but when I cross in front of the television, his head moves to the side so that he doesn't miss any of his program.

Charlie is already in the kitchen, pouring hot chocolate into three mugs.

"Marshmallows?" she asks, and I nod.

She drops a pink marshmallow onto the top of each mug. Then she pauses for a moment, looks at me and plops a second marshmallow onto one of the cups and slides it toward me.

"Thank you," I tell her, picking up the mug.

Charlie walks over and puts a mug of hot chocolate down on the table in front of the boy on the couch.

"This is my brother, Ben," she says.

Ben doesn't look away from the television.

Charlie passes him the remote control. Ben takes it gingerly and flips through a few channels, then settles on one showing a family who cook ridiculously oversized food. There is a little girl with brown curls laughing as she adds a huge cherry to the top of the world's biggest ice cream sundae. It is something Lavender would pick to watch. It's hard to tell, but I think Ben and Lavender could be about the same age.

Ben reaches over and takes a wet wipe from a packet on the table and scrubs at his fingertips where he has touched the remote. He does this three or four times, until he has a neat little pile of used wet wipes on the table in front of him. Then he takes one more and wipes down the handle of the mug and around the lip of it. Only then does he pick up his drink and take a sip.

"Come on, Felix, and I'll show you my room," says Charlie, grabbing a mug of hot chocolate for herself from the counter and walking down toward the back of the boat.

Charlie's entire bedroom is smaller than a single bed. Her actual bed, which is much thinner than a normal bed, takes up most of the available space in the room, but there is a tiny bit of room to walk around the edge of her bed. The walls at the head and foot of her bed have shelves built into them and there are books, gadgets and trinkets filling every surface. One shelf is dedicated just to holding all of her woolly hats, fancy headbands, knitted scarves and leg warmers. Another shelf is stacked high with comic books.

"How come I haven't seen Ben at school?" I ask Charlie, as we sit down on the bed.

"He won't go," says Charlie. "See him wiping his hands before? Well, he is so worried about getting dirty that he pretty much never leaves home unless he absolutely has to. He has a lot of rules, just like you."

"So he never goes to school?" I ask.

I'm sure my face isn't disguising my surprise.

"Like never ever?"

I can't believe that someone wouldn't go to school.

"He used to go," says Charlie. "But then it got too much. He was spending most of his time at school washing his hands, over and over again. He wouldn't touch anything that the other children had touched, which meant that he wouldn't join in any activities in class and he wouldn't play with anyone at break time. If someone touched something of his, he would have a total meltdown. Eventually it just got too hard, so now he just stays at home."

We sit there in silence for a moment, then Charlie reaches down under her bed and pulls out a small, thin book.

"I made you this," says Charlie and she hands the book to me.

It's more of a booklet really, made from brown paper shopping bags that have been cut down to make pages that are all stapled together on one side. Where the bags have writing printed on them, saying the names of the shops they came from, Charlie has stuck heavy white paper over the top, making the pages thick and sturdy.

On the cover there is a bright starburst that says "The Adventures of Rool Boy" in big block letters. Out of the middle of a big puff of smoke there is a superhero flying through the sky. He has brown hair, a gold cape, and is wearing red glasses, just like mine.

"But I thought you couldn't read?" I say.

Charlie smiles. "I'm a really bad reader and my spelling is terrible, but luckily for me, comic books have a lot of pictures. See for yourself."

I turn to the first page. It is filled with colored pictures and letters grouped together to make words.

She's right, the spelling is absolutely awful, but as I begin to read it out loud, the words sound right.

There's a knock on the door and a woman sticks her head in. She's short and thin, with the same bright-red hair as Charlie and a scrape of chocolate icing on her face.

"Hello, love," says Charlie's mom. "You must be Felix."

She holds out her hand. I shake it; up and down, one and two.

"You can call me Jasmine.

"I hate to interrupt your fun, Charlie," Jasmine continues. "But there are a few cakes that need to be delivered to one of the houses on Station Street. Would you mind running them over there on your bike for me?"

Charlie nods, then tips her mug upside down. What's left of the pink marshmallow slides along the edge of the mug and plops into her mouth.

"Come on, Felix," she says and slides off the bed.

She grabs a knitted hat from the cupboard. It is covered in little strings of yarn and looks like a lion's mane.

"You can help."

Her mom smiles. "Thanks, love. I'll pop some nibble pies in the oven and they will be ready when you get back for a bit of an afternoon snack."

There are four large cakes sitting on cooling racks. They take up most of the table space in the tiny galley kitchen, but they smell delicious. There is a chocolate one covered in shiny red cherries, a pink one sprinkled with coconut, one with pale-yellow icing and another covered in sugar daisies.

I watch as Charlie's mom carefully places each one into a cardboard box, then we stack them up in the basket of Charlie's bike.

"What are the cakes for?" I ask, as we wind our way back along the bike path by the river and up to the road.

"Mom bakes them," she says. "It's her job. She normally sells them at the market in the square, but these ones must be a special order."

"Her job is making cakes?"

Charlie nods and turns the bike into Station Street.

"Mom used to own a tea shop and would make these amazing afternoon teas. You know the kind – tiers of tiny cakes on stands, pastries, tarts, and cookies. But with Ben being sick and then not going to school, she couldn't be spending all day at work with him just by himself at home. So she closed the tea shop and used the money to buy this boat. It's the cheapest house around because we didn't have to buy any land for it. And now she makes cakes to sell at the markets in each town we stop in until we get caught by the mooring permit inspectors."

"Mooring permit inspectors?"

"To park our boat. Annual permits are too expensive, so we just park and see how long we can stay before they tell us we have to move on.

Sometimes we only get a couple of days, but we were in the last place for four months before they finally told us we'd have to move. It was great."

"And that's why you've been to so many schools," I say.

It was all starting to make sense to me.

Charlie pulls her bike up in front of a fancy green-colored house toward the end of Station Street.

"Wait here, I won't be a minute," she says and she lifts the cakes from her basket and expertly carries the stack of boxes up the path to the front door.

A minute later she's back with a fistful of cash instead of four boxes of cakes. She shoves the money into her pocket and zips it up carefully before expertly turning the bike back toward home.

When we arrive back at the boat, Jasmine is ready and waiting for us with two plates, each with three little warm meat pies on it. Charlie hands her mother the money from the cakes, then, while we each hold a plate, her mother squeezes tomato sauce onto the top of each pie – heart shaped for Charlie and smiley faces for me.

While cicadas begin to sing in the background, we sit together on the concrete edge of the river, our legs dangling down toward the water, and eat. It doesn't take long until there are ducks quacking all around us. We pick bits off the crust of our pies and see who can throw them the farthest. It is hard to tell who wins each time because the pieces barely touch the water before a duck gobbles them up. I think actually it might be the ducks that are winning.

Charlie finishes first and throws her last bit of crust into the water. After a squabble, a very large duck with green feathers wins it and swims off with it in his beak. I brush the crumbs off my trousers and follow Charlie back inside.

There are a surprising number of hidden cupboards in the boat. Charlie points them out to me when we return.

"We don't have any shelves because when the boat rocks, all of the things would just fall off. Everything has to go away in a cupboard," she explains.

In the family room, Charlie sits down next to Ben on the couch. He is busy watching television and barely seems to notice as Charlie pulls out a drawer that is covered with fabric to look like it is part of the couch. The drawer is full of balls of yarn. Charlie selects a pale pink ball.

"Pick a color, Felix," she says and I reach in and pull out a ball of fluffy orange yarn, then sit down on a worn looking armchair.

"Do you know how to finger knit?" Charlie asks me.

I shake my head.

"It sounds hard," I say.

She grins. "I think it is like learning anything new. It is hard at first, then you do it more and it becomes easy. Watch."

126

Charlie holds out her fingers and quickly wraps a loop of pink yarn around each of them, going from back to front each time, then repeating the process so each finger has two loops instead of just one. Next, she pulls the bottom loop up and over the top of her finger and drops it off the back of her hand. She does this for all of the loops then uses the thread to create a second loop on each finger once more. Over and over she repeats this process and within minutes, she has a small knitted scarf trailing from the back of her hand.

"OK, Felix, it's your turn to try," she says and she pulls all of the loops off her fingers and drops the entire scarf onto the couch.

Charlie shows me how to loop the yarn around my fingers and how to pull the bottom loop up and over the top of my finger. She does the first few rows, then it is my turn to try. I carefully pull each loop over as she has shown me, then re-loop the yarn around each finger. I have to really concentrate, but gradually I begin to get the hang of it.

"That's it," says Charlie. "You're doing it!"

She picks up her own knitting and slips her fingers back into it, picking up easily from where she left off.

I stop what I'm doing for a moment and allow myself a small celebratory smile. She's right. I'm doing it. Then I stop to itch my nose and when I look down again, I can't remember which finger I'm up to in the pattern. As I'm trying to figure it out, two of the loops fall off my fingertips. They get jumbled up with the rest of the orange yarn and I can't find them again. I try to just keep adding new loops to my fingers, but soon my knitting is just in a huge mess.

I pull all of the loops off my fingers and throw my tangled yarn onto the floor in frustration. I can feel my cheeks beginning to get hot as my brain starts to fill with blizzard. I start to get a bad feeling in my stomach and my chest starts to feel all tight.

"I can't do it," I say. "I've messed it all up."

Ben looks over momentarily from his television program, then turns back to watch the screen once more.

"You're still learning," says Charlie. "And finger knitting is easy to learn because … look!"

She removes the pink loops of yarn from her fingers once more and pulls on the string that attaches her knitting to the ball of yarn. Her knitting begins to unravel, loop by loop, row by row until she is just left with the very first loop pinched between her forefinger and thumb. She has just undone her entire scarf in the space of about 10 seconds.

"See?" she says. "You can undo it and do it again until it is just right. And every time you do it again, you're practicing and getting better at it."

She reaches down and picks up my orange mess of knitting and holds it out to me. I pull on the string that attaches it to the ball of yarn and my knitting just un-knits itself like Charlie's did. She shows me how to wind the yarn back onto the ball and helps me to get started again. One, two, three, four. First finger, second finger, third then fourth. It is both stressful and relaxing. It takes up all of my concentration and I'm worried that I might make a mistake, but it has a pleasing rhythm to it.

Before we realize how much time has really passed, the fading light of dusk begins to encircle the boat. Charlie ties off her length of pink knitting and shows me how to do the same. Her knitting is much longer and neater than mine, but I'm still very pleased with mine. I hold it between my thumb and forefinger and wriggle it back and forth. Charlie giggles.

"You just need to add some black stripes to it and you've got a tiger's tail," she says.

I turn around and tuck it into the back of my trousers. It doesn't quite hang down to the back of my knees, but it definitely could be a tiger's tail with some black lines added on.

While Charlie goes up to start unlocking her bike to give me a lift home, I run back to her bedroom to pick up the comic book she made me. It is still sitting open on the bed where I left it before we went to deliver the cakes.

I tuck the comic book under my arm and head back down the hallway.

An everywun cheared. Whn the poole was lled wit custard, everyone from raund the neybahood jumpt in and had fun. Even Rool Boy injoyed himself. Thay hid races an custid ghts. Everywun sed that swiming poole ar beter wen thay ar lled wit water, butt custid woz fun for a chanje - jus this wunce.

As I walk back past Ben and up the stairs to the front deck to leave, I can't help but look back at him.

There is an uneasy feeling about seeing him sitting there alone and pale faced that I just can't shake. He could easily be me. Not the hand wiping, cleaning, and worrying about germs, but the problems that come with having to stick to a set of your own rules. We seem to have a lot of the same problems because of our quite different rules.

This thought whizzes around in my brain most of the way home and I am only jolted back to reality when Charlie pulls her bike up with a skid at my front gate. She helps me out of the sidecar.

"Thanks for having me over," I tell her.

I undo the buckle on my helmet and hand it back.

"That's OK," she says. "Maybe next weekend, I can come over to your place instead."

"Really?" I say. "Would you want to?"

Charlie smiles. "Of course. That's what friends do, Felix. They take turns at sharing."

"So we are friends now?" I ask Charlie.

I think we might be, but I like things to be clear.

"Of course we are," she replies and rolls her eyes at me.

She puts one foot on a pedal and lets the bike coast down the driveway and onto the road as she swings her other leg over and onto the bike.

"You're so funny, Felix. Don't you know we have been friends all along?"

Twenty

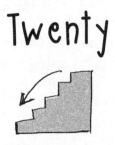

I am still on top of the world when I arrive at school on Monday. Charlie and I are friends. Officially, we are actual, real friends. I've even borrowed some early readers from Lavender so I can start teaching Charlie to read. The books are a bit boring and repetitive, but I'm sure once she has the hang of words like cat, sat, and mat then we can move on to mastering more interesting words like thingamabob, beanpole, and antidisestablishmentarianism, which is the longest word that I know and has 28 letters actually.

I'm so excited about how things are going with Charlie and me being friends that it doesn't even bother me that I have an appointment to see Hugo after break. Instead, I practically skip into his office.

With every visit to see Hugo, I feel like I'm coming away a bit stronger and a bit better at standing up to Basil. Hugo seems to be obsessed with making me do things that Basil doesn't want me to do. Like last week, he made me sit at his computer and type every uneven number up to 99, then back down again. The visit before that, I had to read aloud all of these articles from the newspaper and we talked about how they couldn't possibly all be caused by odd numbers. Hugo even seems to have Mrs. Green on board. She is taking great delight in putting me into groups of three or five when we are doing small group work and I'm getting better at telling Basil that it will all be OK and not getting all upset about it like he tells me to.

Today, Hugo and I are taking on the stairs and there are 11 steps between me and the upper floor. I've counted them many times over my years at Scribbly Gum.

"OK, Felix," says Hugo, "Let's do it."

We are standing at the bottom of the stairs between the preschool corridor and the kindergarten classrooms. As we have spent more and more time together, we have moved beyond just practicing fighting back against Basil in Hugo's room.

"Shall I go first?" asks Hugo. "Or would you like to do it together?"

He is wearing a blue shirt with a polka-dot tie, along with his usual pair of suit shorts. He has switched his black work shoes for a pair of brightly colored sneakers and is dancing about a bit in them, like a runner preparing for the starting gun of a big race.

"Maybe you could go first?"

Hugo nods. He jumps up onto the first step.

"One," he says.

Then he steps up onto the next step and the next one.

"Two, three, four, five, six, seven, eight," he continues. "Nine, ten, and eleven!"

The last number he calls from the top step and gives me a thumbs-up.

"You can do it, Felix. Climb all of the way to the top and step on every single step. Don't skip any, just because they're odd."

The stairs loom large in front of me.

I take a deep breath and lift my right foot. Every part of my being wants to skip the first step and go straight on to the second one. My foot lingers in midair over the first step and I'm standing there teetering on one leg. My leg wants to go on, but Basil pipes up in my head and says *Do you really think this is a good idea? If you step on that step, who knows what might happen? You will probably be knocked over by a car on the way home.*

I put my foot back down again.

"You can do it, Felix," says Hugo.

He's hopping from one foot to the other on the top step and smiling down at me. I think about Charlie being my friend and the excitement of the weekend.

I lift my foot up and carefully place it onto the first step. All I want to do is take it off and put it back onto the ground. Step one is not a good place to be. Then again, I don't want to end up like Charlie's brother, Ben. He's so worried about so many things that it stops him from even going to school.

You can't do it, says Basil. *It will be bad. So bad.* Basil isn't messing around today.

I hold my breath and step on every single step all of the way up. When I get to the top, instead of feeling good, I feel awful. What have I done? Why didn't I follow the rules? I try to placate Basil by jumping twice on the spot at the top of the staircase; it does nothing to stop him howling away in my head.

"Great, Felix," says Hugo, full of enthusiasm. "Let's do it again."

He runs down the stairs to the bottom then turns around and runs back up again.

"Come on, Felix."

I shake my head. I don't want to do it again, but I don't want to be like this forever either. I'm stuck.

My head is spinning with conflict. Part of me wants to do what Hugo wants me to do. I know that is the right thing because it will help me to beat Basil the bully inside my head. Part of me wants to give in to Basil because he is trying to do what is right for me and he is trying to keep me safe. Part of me is worried about becoming like Ben, stuck at home in front of the television all day and being too afraid to leave the house. Then there is part of me that is worried about how school is going and part of me that is worried about what will happen when The Bump arrives as an actual baby and part of me that is worried about staying friends with Charlie because she is the first real friend that I've ever actually had and suddenly all of these worries are spinning around and around in my head.

As my eyes begin to fill with tears, I sit down on the top step with a bump.

Hugo runs up the steps and sits down next to me.

"Felix – what's wrong?" he asks. "You just did so well. You should be happy, not upset."

He seems confused.

I shake my head. It isn't the stairs. I'm sure like getting past having to say hello twice, the stairs are something that I can get past if I work on it hard enough. But where will it end? Will there always be something else that will trigger Basil and set him off? I think about Charlie's brother who now doesn't even leave the boat unless he really, really has to.

"Will I ever get better? Will I ever change?" I ask Hugo. "Or am I going to be like this forever?"

Hugo is quiet for a moment and then he says, "You know what? I don't know the answer to that."

He puts a hand on my shoulder.

"The brain is a very complicated thing, Felix," he says. "And it can be unwell, just like you can skin your knee or have a stomachache. But there are lots of things we can do to help people with a mental illness, just like you.

"Plus what I do know is that we are doing the very best that we can for you and every time you practice standing up to Basil, you're getting stronger and better at it. You're already so much better at it, Felix. You just have to keep working at it."

Hugo smiles at me. His eyes are warm and kind.

"But what if he never goes away? What if I have Basil in my head forever?"

Hugo shrugs.

"He might be there forever, Felix. But he doesn't need to be a big, strong Basil who tells you what to do and completely takes over your life. He could just be there as a little sprout, a little leaf. And you're definitely strong enough to be the boss of a little sprout. You won't let a bully like Basil tell you what to do."

I nod, slowly.

Hugo stands up and holds out his hands. I give him mine and he pulls me back up to my feet.

"Let's have another try, Felix. Let's stand up to Basil."

• • •

Charlie and I are sitting on the log in our usual break time positions and I've been teaching her all of the sounds that letter A can make using one of the early reading books.

"So this one is 'a' like cat, there's 'a' like in day and it can also make an 'ah' sound like the end of Australia," says Charlie, her brow furrowed.

Learning to read in English is a very complicated business as it turns out.

"Hey, want to come and join our game? We are playing Knockout."

My lesson is interrupted by Samira Chen carrying a basketball.

Charlie looks at me for permission and I shrug.

"One letter is probably enough for today," I tell her.

Charlie closes the reader and slides down off the log.

"Come on then, Felix. Let's play."

I see Samira hesitate for a moment, like she is going to say that I'm not invited.

Samira's eyes look at Charlie, then at me, then flick back at Charlie. It's like she's weighing the situation up in her mind. She wants Charlie to play, but she thinks I'm going to ruin the game with my rules. I understand what she is thinking. It has happened so many times before. Samira throws the ball back and forth between her hands, like she's juggling, but with just one huge ball instead of three little ones.

Finally, she looks at me, cautiously.

"Felix, you could come and play too, if you like."

I have absolutely no idea what "Knockout" is, but I nearly fall off the log and knock myself out in surprise at being included. I thought she was going to leave me behind. I shove the reader into my schoolbag and slide down off the log.

We both follow Samira over to the basketball court. Maisie and Daisy are already there and so are Tim and Marco from the other class. Samira stands in front of the basketball hoop and the others line up behind her. I join the end of the line and watch carefully.

Samira shoots the basketball up toward the basket and gets it in. She passes the ball to Maisie and runs to the back of the line. Maisie shoots and misses, then the ball is passed to Tim.

"Hang on," I say and the game stops.

I see the twins roll their eyes at each other and Samira takes a deep breath.

"What, Felix?" she says, clearly thinking that I am about to stop the game to add a rule or two of my own.

"I was just wondering what happens now?" I ask.

"Oh," pops out of her mouth, like a little gasp of surprise. "Well, because Maisie missed her shot, she has to go and wait to the side of the basket. That's called 'in limbo.' If Tim gets his shot in, then Maisie is out. If Tim misses, then Maisie is safe and she gets to join the back of the line and then Tim is in limbo."

Tim misses his shot, so Maisie is safe and returns to the line. Daisy scores, so Tim is out, then it's Charlie's turn. She hits the backboard, then the rim of the basket, but the ball doesn't go through the hoop. She then has to wait "in limbo." Marco shoots next and scores, so, according to Samira who is now commentating every shot of the game to me, Charlie is out.

Charlie steps aside and Marco passes me the ball. I step up to the line and throw the ball at the basket, trying to copy what the others did. It is not at all surprising that I miss by a mile. In fact, the ball doesn't even get close to the ring or the backboard. Instead, it sails through the air and hits the back fence of the basketball court so hard that it then rolls back to me and lands at my feet. The others all giggle.

At first, I'm embarrassed. I can feel my cheeks flush red.

They're going to kick you out of the game for sure, says Basil with certainty. *You should get out of here. Run away, Felix. Run away.*

I turn around, planning my escape. My heart begins to pound in my chest and I can feel my breath starting to quicken.

"Haven't you ever shot a basketball before?" asks Maisie, picking up the ball and walking over to me.

I shake my head. *They're on to me. They'll never want to play with me now.*

"Here," says Maisie. "Have another shot."

Basil, who is spoiling for a fight in my head, is thrown off track. *They should be mad at you,* he says. *You're hopeless. Just run off and leave them to play in peace.*

Maisie throws the ball gently back to me.

"Hold your hands like this," Maisie instructs and she puts her hands up in the air.

I do my best to copy her, ignoring the voice of Basil in my head.

"It's not like that," says Daisy, cutting in. "It's more like this."

Daisy stands beside me and puts her hands into a similar position to Maisie's. The difference between the two positions is hard to tell. Tim, Marco, and Samira join them and soon all of the others are standing around with their hands in

funny positions in the air, trying to teach me how to shoot a basket.

It takes me four more shots to get one in and when I do they all cheer and pat me on the back. Then they spend the next minute arguing about whose advice helped me to score my first basket.

It is Charlie who suggests that we should maybe get back to the game. We have time for five more rounds before the bell finally goes for the end of lunch. I get out first time and every time, but I truly don't care.

"Want to play again tomorrow?" says Charlie.

The twins link arms with me and we all walk back toward the classroom to line up. There are so many feelings and emotions swirling around in my head that I'm not sure I even know what to say to describe how I'm feeling.

Eventually, there are just two words that come to mind so I use them.

"Yes, please."

Twenty-Two

Every morning break time, I teach Charlie a new set of sounds. Then every lunch break, we join a game of Knockout and it is actually very fun. She's getting really good at reading the early readers and I'm getting really good at Knockout. Well, not really good, but definitely better than I used to be. Some of the other kids from Mrs. Green's class join in too, and, yesterday, we even had a game with everyone in the class playing at once. I was not even the first one to go out. Gerund O'Toole was too busy trying to show off and missed the ring completely, then Charlie made a basket and knocked him out of the game. It was completely exciting.

There aren't many things in Knockout that upset Basil either. Like there is no keeping score, so there is no chance that I'll get an odd number which could easily go badly. And that is good because the other kids from Mrs. Green's class have been happier to have me join in the game now too. I'm feeling a bit more confident that I can stand up to Basil now and join in without worrying as much about whether I'll have some kind of meltdown and end up throwing the basketball into a trash can (which actually happened several times in Year Three).

In fact, I've been feeling so good about controlling Basil that Hugo gave me a special mission to complete at home: to help Dad redecorate the family room which he has been desperate to do for ages. We have lived here for several years now and he hasn't been able to change so much as a light bulb without me making a fuss. When I suggest to him that Hugo says we should paint the family room, Dad's face lights up like I've just told him that today is Christmas Day.

"Really?" he asks. "Are you sure, Felix?"

But you like things as they are, says Basil. I ignore Basil and nod my head at Dad.

"I could even help you if you like."

Why would you want to do that? scoffs Basil. *Keep it the same. It's safer. If you change it, something bad will happen. I'm sure of it.*

I grit my teeth. I think about all of the things that Hugo and I have practiced to block Basil out. "Yes, Dad. Let's do it," I tell him.

Dad jumps up from the table and dashes out to his shed, returning a minute later with drop cloths, brushes, rollers, and the can of paint that he had picked out earlier.

I help him to drag the furniture away from the

wall, put down the cloths to cover the floor and pick up a brush. The holes have already been filled and the edges already taped off from before, so we can get started straightaway. Within an hour, the family room looks completely different. Dad is happy with it. Basil is not happy with it, but I'm able to tell him that I think it is really all right.

Even Mrs. Lovejoy at school seems more positive. She actually smiled at me the other day, which I had never experienced before, then she started whistling as she walked away along the hallway.

I should have known that it was all too good to last, especially after I heard the whistling.

This morning, we have been reading *Bridge to Terabithia*. It is literacy hour after all, so reading it is definitely the right thing to be doing. I'm up to the part where Leslie and Jess swing over the dry creek bed for the first time and create Terabithia. It is their very own place, a special place, just like Narnia or Neverland.

I'm pretty sure that Charlie is reading a comic book inside her copy of *Bridge to Terabithia* as usual. I'm not sure that she definitely is because I am doing my best to ignore her because what she is doing is not the right thing to do and I know that once I know she isn't doing the right thing, I'll find it very hard to ignore it. Or rather, Basil will find it hard to ignore it. So I've worked out that it is best if I just don't know some things.

Gerund O'Toole, however, is clearly not going to let it go unnoticed. He is definitely still annoyed about the fact that Charlie got him out of the game of Knockout yesterday.

He leans back on his chair and reaches behind Charlie's book. Before she can stop him, he has grabbed her comic book.

"What's with the picture book?" says Gerund.

He rocks forward on his chair and flips through the worn pages. They are a blur of bright colors and speech bubbles.

"I just like them, that's all," Charlie says. Her cheeks flush pink.

She reaches forward to take back the comic, but Gerund whips it away before she can reach it.

"Can I have it back, please?"

He shakes his head.

"I'm not done with it yet," he says and takes out his pen.

He begins to add little details to the pictures. Within moments, the flying superhero on the cover has bolts in the side of his head like Frankenstein's monster, a lightning shaped scar like Harry Potter, and an angel halo hovering above his head. Gerund then turns his attention to the first page.

And that's when I realize it. Charlie is my friend. And friends don't let other friends get pushed around. Not by anyone. Especially not by Gerund O'Toole.

"Hey!" I say to Gerund.

I stand up and step between his desk and Charlie's.

"Why don't you just leave her alone?"

Gerund looks up at me in surprise.

"And… and… give her book back," I add, trying to make my voice sound tough and full of authority, but I'm not sure that it comes out that way. I actually sound more like Henry grunting like a gorilla.

Gerund just snorts, then laughs and carries on doodling.

What can I say to make him change his mind? I desperately want him to know that pushing my friend around is not OK. Then, suddenly, I've got it.

"It is OK that she looks at comics, you know. In fact, I think it is really cool," I say.

Charlie smiles at me, encouragingly, so I plow on.

"She likes them because she can't read. They help her because they don't have too many words, but they have lots of pictures."

At that moment, the noise in the classroom suddenly evaporates and it is silent.

You could hear a pencil drop. Everyone stares at me and then at Charlie.

The smile disappears from her face and is replaced by a look of complete horror.

"Still learning to read?" Gerund says, with a smirk. "What are you? Five?"

Charlie's cheeks go from pink to a flaming red to match her hair.

Some of the others kids start to giggle and snigger. I see a few of them exchange looks with each other that clearly say that they think she's weird for not being able to read.

"Felix!" she says. "Why would you tell everyone that? I thought we were friends."

Charlie pushes her chair back from her desk, snatches her comic out of Gerund's hands and runs from the classroom as quickly as her legs will carry her. Mrs. Green looks up from her desk just in time to see the tip of Charlie's bright red ponytail as she streaks through the doorway and out of the room.

I didn't mean to embarrass her. I was trying to help.

I want to run down the corridor after her, but Mrs. Green fixes me with a gaze that clearly says, "If you so much as think about causing any trouble, Felix, I'm going to call Mrs. Lovejoy." I know that if I run after her I'll be out of Scribbly Gum Primary without so much as a "See you later!" on my way out.

I sit back down at my desk, but I can feel everyone's eyes on me as I try to continue with my work. Mrs. Green sends Maisie to see if Charlie is OK and Maisie reports back that she has found her in the bathroom and that she is just washing her face. The job of washing her face seems to take the rest of the lesson.

At break time, I eat my snack on my log. Nobody from Grade Six is playing any games today. They're all too busy gossiping about what just happened in class. A Grade Six girl not being able to read is unheard of at Scribbly Gum Primary. Eventually, I see Charlie squeeze out a side door at the end of the building. Almost immediately, Gerund O'Toole is upon her. Even from my spot on the log I can hear him as he prances around her singing the alphabet song that we learned in our first year of school, the one that teaches you all of the letters. That song is really for little kids. You know, the ones that can't even read yet. When Gerund reaches the end of the song, he continues his prancing and starts taunting her in a baby voice.

"You should be in the little kids' playground," he says. "If you need help reaching the water fountain, just let us know."

While all of this is happening, the girls that we usually play with ignore Charlie, like she is not even there, and the boys seem to be really concentrating on trying to spin basketballs on their fingertips while also ignoring what is going on.

When Charlie walks past the log, I reach out and grab the sleeve of her red school shirt.

"Charlie," I say, "I'm sorry."

Gerund, who is still following Charlie, repeats exactly what I just said using the same baby voice.

"Oh push off, Gerund," she says. "Go and annoy someone else."

Gerund laughs and runs off toward the basketball court.

"I know you didn't mean to embarrass me, Felix," says Charlie, turning to face me. "I know you were trying to be helpful. It's just now everyone is talking about me, making fun of me and laughing about me."

"But they're not. I don't think anyone is talking about you," I say.

This is clearly not true. We both turn and look over at the groups of Grade Six students scattered about the playground. As if on cue, the moment we look at them, they immediately stop their conversations and look away, all pretending that something on the ground is suddenly very interesting.

"I gave you a secret to look after, Felix, and you shared it with everyone," Charlie says. "Now everyone is treating me like I have something that might be contagious. I'm so embarrassed and I just need some time by myself."

She walks away over to the monkey bars, pulls herself up onto the highest rungs and sits there by herself. I want to go over, but I think the reception would be so frosty that it could turn water to ice in seconds. I spend the rest of break time on my log, all by myself, except for Basil who points out that this is all my fault.

I'm the first one in line at the end of lunch. Mostly because the log is so conveniently located, but also because it is time for our library lesson. A whole hour of uninterrupted time in the library. This is one of my favorite times of the week. It is my happy hour and it is a time that I feel like I can just relax and forget all of my problems at school.

The other kids trickle in slowly, shoving lunch boxes and drink bottles away in their bags. I'm the first one lined up outside the classroom ready to go with my library bag when the bell rings.

Once we are all lined up, Miss Claudette, with her jangly bangles and colorful headscarves usually collects us and takes us over to the library for our lesson. When I see Mrs. Green coming along the hallway instead, I already know that there must be a problem. I can just tell from the look on her face that she knows that I'm not going to be happy about what she has to say.

"Our library lesson has been canceled for this afternoon. There is an African music group that has come to visit, so all of the classes from Year Three to Six are going to watch them perform in the hall instead of their usual lessons."

I shake my head. I don't want to go to see some traveling music show. I want to go to my library lesson. My heart begins to pound in my chest. It feels like it might jump right out.

And now is the right time for library, says Basil.

You should be going to the library.

I know and I don't even bother to argue against Basil. Instead, I agree with him.

"It's OK, Felix. I'll organize with Miss Claudette for the class to have a makeup library lesson so you won't miss out altogether," says Mrs. Green.

"No!" I shout at her. "That's not all right. We should be having our lesson now."

The rest of the class shrinks away from me as I yell and stamp my feet. Even Mrs. Green takes a step back.

So make it right, urges Basil. *Go to your library lesson!*

It's a good idea. Before I can stop myself, I've turned around and I'm running off down the hallway. Mrs. Green calls something after me, but I'm a man on a mission. Nobody is going to stop me from going to the library this afternoon. I'll just tell Miss Claudette that I need to come to the library instead of the performance. That it is important. She'll understand. She will let me stay in the library instead of making me go to see the musical Africans.

I run across the asphalt and up the steps of the library two at a time. I grab the handle on the library door and pull. Nothing happens. I try again, but the door is locked. I shake the handle frantically, but it is definitely locked. Miss Claudette must have closed the library to go to the performance. No!

I look around for another way to get in and an

open window catches my eye. It is closer to the roof than it is to the ground and it is about the size of a suitcase. I drop my schoolbag on the steps and run over so I'm just underneath the window. I try jumping up to grab the sill with my fingertips, but I'm just a bit too short to reach it. I clamber onto a nearby bush, trying to get some extra height, but the branches are too flimsy and just bend down to the ground under my weight.

Go, Felix, go! says Basil, urgently. *You're doing the right thing. The library is the right place to be on a Thursday afternoon.*

I abandon the bush in favor of pulling over a bench from a nearby outdoor seating area. It is heavy and makes a loud scraping noise as I drag it across the pavement. Once it is under the window I'm able to jump up and grab on to the windowsill.

With some serious effort, I'm able to squeeze myself through the gap between the glass and the frame, and wriggle the top half of my body through so I'm draped over the windowsill, half in and half out of the library. I have to pause at this point and have a rest.

Breaking into the library is actually very tiring work. I'm sure it would look pretty funny with my legs just dangling there by themselves on the outside of the building. Once I've caught my breath, I stretch forward with my arms and shimmy the rest of my body up and through the window. I feel myself beginning to slither forward and look down in time to see that the window is very conveniently located above a pile of beanbags. I land gently cushioned by millions of tiny beanbag beans, that make a very quiet "tch" noise as I tumble onto them with legs and arms going everywhere.

Yes! says Basil. *You're here.* He begins to calm down.

The lights are off inside the library, but there is something comforting about the cool, semi-darkness. I brush myself off and head straight for the carts behind the desk. I didn't come in to help Miss Claudette at lunchtime, so I know that there are plenty of books waiting to be put away.

After I file all of the books back on the shelves, I run my hands along the spines to make sure they are all sitting evenly lined up with each other. I look around to see what else needs doing. I wipe down all of the tables with a cloth and tuck all of the chairs in underneath, arranging them so they are equal distance apart. I take all of the pencils out of their cups. One by one, I poke them into the electric pencil sharpener so they are all sharpened to a point, then I put them back so each cup has one of each color. I straighten the rug, plump the two cushions on Miss Claudette's chair, and clean the whiteboard for her. Finally, I grab the feather duster and run it over every surface in the library. It takes ages, but by the time I'm finished, it looks great.

Normally, coming to work in the library gives me a feeling of peacefulness, a sort of inner calm. Today, even after doing every job that I can possibly think of, I still don't feel relaxed. It is hard to describe what I am feeling. It is like having butterflies in your stomach, fluttering around, but then also wearing boots that are filled with concrete. Like on one hand I feel jittery and jumpy, while on the other hand I am heavyhearted. Even after restoring order to everything around me, I still have an unsettled feeling.

And I still can't shake it when I unlock the library door to let myself out, just before the final bell at the end of the day. I pick up my schoolbag from the steps and walk straight into Mrs. Lovejoy.

"Felix!" she says. "There you are."

I look at her. She looks cross. Mega cross.

"Hello, Mrs. Lovejoy. Hello, Mrs. Lovejoy," I say.

Saying it twice helps me to feel a little bit better, even though I know I'm not supposed to. When I do it, I see a frown cross Mrs. Lovejoy's face. I'm still filled with the worried feeling that I get when something isn't right, when something bad is going to happen.

"Quite a few teachers have been looking for you," says Mrs. Lovejoy.

She purses her lips and crosses her arms. Her suit jacket rustles angrily.

"Have they?" I say. "I've just been helping out in the library."

I sidestep around her to continue on my way. I don't even go back to the classroom to collect my things. I just want to get home as quickly as possible. Mrs. Lovejoy shouts after me, but I pretend like I can't hear her. If she wants to expel me from school, she will just have to wait until tomorrow.

It's Thursday and that is the day that I walk home and when I get home, I get to have Mom all to myself for an hour or so while everyone else is off at their activities. When I get to the school gate, I'm surprised to see our car parked just out front with Lavender already getting in.

That isn't right, says Basil. *Lavender goes to art class on Thursday afternoon. Mrs. Jenkins takes her with Annabelle.*

I try to shush Basil, but as soon as I pull the door open, I know he is right. This is definitely all wrong.

For one thing, Dad is driving and he never collects us from school. I'm surprised that he even knows where to come to collect us. He's usually so busy chopping up people's houses to come to school pickups and drop-offs. We put our schoolbags into the trunk and climb into the car. For another thing, Alice and Henry are already in the car and Mom never picks them up first. Plus, everyone is quiet and in my family, nobody is ever quiet.

"Where's Mom?" asks Lavender.

She always gets the middle seat because she is the smallest.

"Is it the baby?"

Dad runs his hands through his hair. That's when I notice that he is still wearing his paint splattered overalls and his shabby steel-capped boots.

"So, kids," he says, turning around in his seat to face us all. "Your mom had the baby this afternoon."

Henry gives a cheerful grunt.

"I knew it!" exclaims Alice.

Lavender claps her hands together in excitement. "Is it a boy or a girl?"

"It's a girl," says Dad.

Alice and Lavender squeal with delight and clap their hands. Even Henry cracks a grin.

Dad, however, still isn't smiling. You would think

he would be more excited about the new baby. He pauses to look at each of us.

"There's a bit of a problem. She was born early. She wasn't meant to be here for another two months, so she is very small. The doctors aren't sure if she's going to make it. Your mom is with her at the hospital and we are going to go straight there now."

The inside of the car goes completely silent. Even more silent than it was before. It is like the silence begins to fill up the space in the car and the longer that nobody says anything, the bigger it gets until I can almost feel it pushing down on my chest, my heart. The air becomes so thick that you could cut it with a knife, just like cutting a slice of cake.

There is only one voice that I can hear and that's Basil. *This is your fault,* he says. *If you hadn't done all of those things that weren't right. The stairs, the odd numbers, the single hellos, the painting the family room, and all the rest. If you had just stuck to the rules then this never would have happened. Everyone would be safe. You didn't even want there to be another baby and now this has happened.*

It is all your fault, Felix.

I think he is right.

Dad drives us straight to the hospital and nobody says anything the whole way there, except for Lavender sniffling a bit. It is like some kind of

Twain family silence record. I catch myself tapping two fingers on the car window and don't even try to stop myself. Nobody else in the car notices the tapping or if they do, they don't make their usual complaints about it. I try to think about Mom and think about the new baby, but my head is filled with Basil. He is busy telling me that this whole thing is my fault. If only I'd listened to him and stuck to the rules, then everyone in my family would be safe now. None of this would be happening.

When I think about all of the things that I have been doing over the last few weeks that have upset Basil, I feel sick. By the time we reach the hospital, I know that there is no way that I can go inside.

"I'll wait out here," I tell Dad when we arrive.

I sit down on a bench by the door of the hospital and cross my arms. Dad looks at me, then at Alice, Lavender, and Henry who are already halfway down the hallway, following those brightly colored lines that are often painted on the floors of hospitals to tell you where to go.

"Are you sure, Felix? I think Mom would like to see you."

"I'm very sure," I say and he turns to follow the others to where Mom is with the new baby.

There is no way that I can go in and see the baby when this whole situation is all my fault.

Twenty-Four

With Dad in charge at home, everything goes completely and utterly wrong. For starters, he wakes us up at completely the wrong time and we are all in a massive rush trying to get ready for school. Henry can't find his sports bag and Lavender can't find one of her tiny silver earrings. Alice is oblivious to the chaos around her and is going through her ballet barre routine at the counter, headphones blaring, one hand on the counter and a slice of toast in the other. Dad is standing in Mom's spot

trying to wrangle sandwiches into ziplock bags. They end up looking very smooshed in there. He puts my breakfast in the wrong spot. It's not my right cereal, it's not my bowl or spoon. And he has already poured milk over it.

Wrong, wrong, wrong, wrong, says Basil. *True, true, true, true,* I tell him.

I abandon breakfast and decide that I need to escape the chaos in the family room. Instead, I slip quietly through the doorway under the stairs and down to check on my ark collection. Just like the half-dark library yesterday, sitting in the cool cellar with my beanbag and well-organized collection is usually calming. I carefully take every ark and every animal off and wipe down the table with my cloth. Then I carefully replace everything back into position, with the arks all lined up at the back of the table and the animals two by two in front. I save the wooden elephant with the broken leg until last.

Even when I've finished the whole process, I still don't feel any better. In the back of my mind, there is still that worried sort of feeling. I can't put my finger on what it is exactly.

Dad's head suddenly appears above me in the doorway.

"Felix! What are you doing?" he says.

He looks cross and his tone is snappy.

"You're not even dressed! We were meant to

leave for school ten minutes ago."

I shake my head. I don't want to go to school today.

"What's wrong?" Dad asks. "You need to go upstairs and get dressed immediately. We're going to be late!"

"Can I please just go to visit Mom instead?"

Dad's face softens and he sighs.

"All right. I'll drop the others at school and I'll come back for you. You need to be ready in 20 minutes."

I wait until I hear the car start in the driveway before I climb up out of my cellar. I'm dressed and waiting by the door with my backpack ready by the time he gets back.

When we get to the hospital, Dad parks the car and we climb out. I make sure to tap the door handle twice. I can't afford for any more things to go wrong. Then we scurry toward the entrance, trying to avoid the rain that has begun to fall. As we get to the sliding doors, I realize that I still can't go in and instead head back to my bench from yesterday. Dad goes inside with the promise of sending Mom out to me.

As I sit there, on my bench under the covered walkway, people pass me and head in and out of the hospital entrance. Some come out and sit on the benches near me, wearing their bathrobes and slippers. Others are clearly going in as visitors, wielding large bunches of flowers and balloons with get well messages on them.

As I watch, Mom comes out through the automatic doors. She looks different and it takes me a moment to realize that it is because she is no longer mostly made up of The Bump. She's back to just Mom again. It has only been two days since I've seen Mom, but it feels much longer. She comes over to join me on the hard bench and gives me a big, squishy hug. I squeeze her tight. She feels soft.

"Don't you want to come in and meet your new sister, Felix?" Mom asks.

I shake my head.

"Is it because she isn't a boy?" says Mom.

I shake my head again, although I hadn't even thought of that. Now I have three sisters and one brother! Three! One! I feel Basil groan as I take in all of the odd numbers.

"It's because it's all my fault," I tell her.

"Don't be silly, Felix," says Mom. "It isn't your fault."

She is speaking softly and when I look at her, I realize that she looks very tired. I want to tell her about Charlie and the secret and our fight and about Basil being bossy again and about breaking the rules and that making the baby arrive too early, but I can tell that she is only half present, sitting here with me. She has too many other things going on right now.

"I tell you what, Felix," says Mom, wearily. "We

haven't given the baby a name yet. And I think that you are just the right person to choose it. But, in order to do that, you'll have to come in and see her. Deal?"

"I'll think about it," I tell Mom.

She hugs me again, then she has to go back inside to the baby. Dad comes down a short time later and we go out for milkshakes and muffins. As we eat, I try to work out what to do.

This is all your fault, says Basil. *You should have been keeping everyone safe.*

The feeling of worry inside me is overwhelming and it is slowly getting bigger. Soon it will be too big for me. Then where will I be? Am I just turning into Charlie's brother, Ben? Working in the library didn't help me. Sorting out my arks didn't help me. Talking to Mom about it didn't help me. I think there is just one person left who can help.

• • •

If Hugo seems surprised to see me at school in casual clothes, he doesn't say anything.

"Hello, Felix," he says. "Come in."

He is sitting at his computer with his shorts and smart shoes. He is wearing a crazy tie today. It is black-and-yellow striped and makes it look like there is a swarm of bumblebees sitting on the front of his shirt.

I sit down on his pink couch, just like I have

so many times before, between a cactus-shaped cushion and one that has shiny gold stripes.

"I'm having some problems," I tell him.

Then I tell him all about accidentally telling everyone about Charlie's secret. And about having trouble standing up to Basil. And about the new baby and how everything is my fault.

Hugo sits and listens to all of it.

Then he says something that surprises me.

"I can't help you anymore, Felix."

I stare at him.

He shrugs his shoulders.

"We have been practicing standing up to Basil in this room together for a long time now. You know what you need to do. I can't get into your brain and do it for you. You're strong enough to overcome him and you need to do that yourself. And it is your friendship with Charlie and only you know what it will take to make it right with her. I can't just hit rewind and take it all back for you. You will need to think of a way to show her that you are sorry for what you said."

Hugo folds his hands in his lap.

I don't know what to say. I thought I would come here and Hugo would help me solve all of my problems. Instead, he is telling me to go away and solve them myself?

I leave Hugo's office not sure what to feel. I'm stunned and surprised that he said he wouldn't help me. I'm proud that he thinks I can stand up to Basil by myself, even though I'm not sure that I can. My brain is full of a whirlwind of thoughts and feelings and ideas.

Out of the corner of my eye, I see Miss Claudette walking across the asphalt, waving at me. I raise my hand and wave back. She is wearing a bright-orange dress and an orange-and-purple scarf tied around her head. As she gets closer, she gives me one of her huge smiles.

"The library has never looked better, Felix," she says when I get closer. "You did a great job."

I let out a tiny smile.

"How did you know it was me?"

Miss Claudette laughs.

"The whole thing had Felix Twain written all over it. It was so obviously your handiwork. I showed it to Mrs. Lovejoy too."

Miss Claudette stops talking and looks at me.

"What's wrong?"

"I just have some problems that I don't know how to solve," I say and sigh.

I thought Hugo was the one person who could help me, but even he is no use.

"Come with me, Felix," she says and I follow her across the asphalt and into the library.

"Wait here," she says.

I stand near her desk while she goes over and rummages about on the shelves. When she returns, she is holding a small book.

It is a thin, shabby hardcover copy of a book called *The Little Prince*. I haven't seen it before.

She begins flipping the pages of the book until it falls open at a page close to the start of the story.

"What do you see when you look at this picture?" says Miss Claudette. She holds up the book for me to see, but I don't need to look closely to know the answer.

"It's a picture of a hat," I tell her.

It's definitely a hat, confirms Basil.

"What if I told you that it is also a picture of a boa constrictor that has eaten an elephant?" she says.

"It can't be that. Because it's a picture of a hat," I say.

Miss Claudette turns the page in the book to show me another drawing. This one definitely looks like a boa constrictor that has swallowed an elephant. I can even see the elephant drawn inside it.

"See? It's the same shape. It really just depends on how you look at it as to what you can see," says Mrs. Claudette.

She chuckles and all of the turquoise bangles on her wrists jangle merrily. She turns the page back and forth so I can see it changing: a hat, then elephant-in-a-boa-constrictor, then a hat, then elephant-in-a-boa-constrictor, then a hat again.

I'm amazed. Both pictures look right, but they can't both be right, can they?

But they are both right, says Basil. *Both of them are right.*

"It is the same thing, just a different way of looking at it," says Miss Claudette. "So maybe you just have to think about your problems in a different way to solve them."

I think about all of my problems. Basil. Mrs. Lovejoy. The kids at school. Mom. The baby. My friendship problem with Charlie. I've tried saying sorry to her, but it just wasn't enough. How could

I show Charlie that I really, truly meant it? That I really was sorry?

I think back over the best bits of our short but promising friendship, then I know exactly what I need to do.

"Miss Claudette, could I please borrow some paper?"

Twenty-Six

It takes me some serious cutting, gluing, writing, drawing, and coloring to put it together. When I'm finished, Miss Claudette helps me to staple the pages in the right order and it is complete.

I wait until the lunch bell rings, then I take my comic book out to the playground. The yard is already full of kids, streaming out of their classrooms into the fresh air. The ground is still damp from the morning showers, but the sun is out now, struggling to make its way out from behind the clouds.

I scan the playground until I see her: Charlie. She is sitting on my log by herself. I guess, technically, it is our log now. It is easy to spot her as she is the only one dressed up like a Dalmatian with black-and-white spotty ears, leg warmers, and a tail. I take a deep breath and walk over.

"Charlie," I say and she turns to look at me. "Can I have a word?"

She nods and I sit down next to her on the log.

"I just wanted to say that I'm really sorry. I didn't mean to tell everyone your secret."

I thrust my freshly made comic book into her hands.

"And I made you this."

"*The Adventures of Really Sorry Boy,*" Charlie reads from the cover and grins. "And I didn't even have to sound it out. I don't think it will be as popular as Superman, but you never know."

I smile. She smiles back.

"Thanks, Felix."

"So are we friends again now? Can we go back to playing together again?" I ask.

My heart is pounding in my chest. I hadn't realized how much this had been weighing on me, making me feel worried and anxious. I thought I was completely fine being by myself.

Charlie shakes her head.

"I'm sorry, Felix. I have some bad news for you. Mom told me that we are moving again."

I stand there, dumbfounded. I knew she moved around a lot, but I just hadn't seen this coming. "But… but… but why?"

"Mom's found a specialist that might be able to help Ben. It would be so great if he could have someone to help him, just like you have had Hugo to help you."

"Well I'm sure Hugo could help Ben," I say, full of hope. "Then you could stay. Let's go and ask him right now."

I slide off the log, ready to run back to Hugo's office, but Charlie grabs my arm.

"Sorry, Felix. We have to go. We need someone who is really specialized and able to come to our place to work with him. Hugo is busy with his work and there are other kids at school here with other problems that need him too."

I nod. I know that she's right. That doesn't make hearing the news any easier though. I'm desperate for her not to leave. I rack my brain for any reason that might be able to keep her from going.

"But what about your reading?" The thought comes to me suddenly. "Surely that is a good enough reason to stay. You're getting so much better and it wouldn't take that much more and you'd be able to do it on your own!"

Charlie's face lights up when I mention how much progress she has made. Her spelling is still pretty awful, but she has been making big improvements. It would be a shame it give it all up now.

"Don't worry about that," she tells me. "I'm so much more confident with it now and that's thanks to you, Felix. Now that I know that I can learn how to do it and that it isn't too late for me, I'll definitely ask someone to help me at my next school."

The bell rings and the playground begins to empty around us.

"I have to go," I tell her and point to my casual clothes. "I'm not really actually meant to be here at school."

Charlie stretches out her arms and gives me a hug. This is another new friendship experience for me. My arms flail around a bit awkwardly before I work out exactly what to do with them. It is an unfamiliar experience. Normally, the only people that hug me are my family and even then, I don't let it happen very often if I can help it.

"Good luck, Felix," she says.

As I turn and walk away, she suddenly chases after me.

"Mrs. Green told us about your baby sister. You know you didn't make that happen, right? It is just one of those things that happens in life. It's just an unfortunate event. But it is absolutely not your fault. Or Basil's fault. It is much bigger than you. It's like fate or destiny or something. It would have happened anyway. It is nothing to do with something that you did or didn't do."

I nod. Is she really right?

"But either way, you should go and see her. You'll regret it if you don't. You could even show her *Rool Boy*."

I smile, trying to picture a tiny baby reading a comic book.

"Maybe I will," I tell her and I run off toward the front gates.

• • •

Dad is there, sitting in the car doing some kind of renovation related paperwork while he waits for me. If he is surprised when I tell him that he needs to drive me back to the hospital, he doesn't show it.

When we get there, I jump out of the car and fling the door shut behind me. This time, there is no touching the door handle.

Touch it twice, says Basil. *You need to stick to the*

rules so nothing bad happens.

I stride on toward the entrance of the hospital, firmly ignoring Basil. As I get closer to the sliding glass doors, I feel the doubts begin to creep in.

"This isn't my fault," I tell myself. "I didn't make this happen."

Yes, you did, says Basil. *You didn't follow the rules and now your family is paying for it.*

"They're not my rules," I tell him.

Of course, they're your rules. Basil is smug. *Who else's rules would they be?*

"They're your rules and I don't have to follow them," I say.

You do too.

"No, I don't. You don't control me anymore, Basil."

My voice is getting louder, stronger.

Do you want awful things to keep happening?

"They might keep happening, but that is out of my control," I tell him. "I can't control what is happening to everyone around me every day just by doing all of the little things you tell me to do the correct number of times. I don't have to listen to you. I'm done."

You're not, says Basil. *You'll never be done.*

"I AM DONE!" I shout the words loudly and clearly.

People on the nearby benches are startled and look at me in alarm. I take several big gulps of air and feel them going all of the way into my lungs. My heart feels light and for the first time in ages, I feel as light as a feather and without a worry in the world.

I'll always be here, says Basil, quietly.

"And I'll always be ready for you," I declare. "But right now, I'm going in to see my sister. And it is definitely the right thing to do."

And with that, I march in through the hospital doors.

It takes me about 20 steps to catch my breath and realize that now that I'm finally inside the building, I don't actually know where I'm going. I feel a bit sheepish as I stand there and wait for Dad to catch up. Then I have to wait while he buys two cups of coffee and some sandwiches to take with us.

When we finally get upstairs, I can see Mom, sitting by a big clear plastic box. Inside, there is a tiny baby, covered in what seems like a dozen tubes and wires all leading away to different machines. She is wearing the world's smallest diaper and a teensy little blue-and-pink knitted hat.

Dad hands Mom a cup of coffee and a sandwich and we all stand around looking at the baby. Every little movement she makes is mesmerizing. Mom tells us that the doctor came around about an hour ago and that they are very pleased with how she is doing.

I dig around in my bag and find the comic book

Charlie made. I hold up Rool Boy so she can see it through the glass.

"This is a comic book that my friend Charlie made for me. She's pretty good at drawing, don't you think? This is my favorite page."

I show her the page where everyone is swimming in the custard swimming pool.

The baby doesn't move, but I'm pretty sure she is impressed.

"Have you thought of a name for her yet, Felix?" Mom asks, between mouthfuls.

I nod. "I was thinking that we could call her Claudette-Charlottina."

Dad snorts and almost spits his mouthful of

coffee out. Mom gives him a withering look.

"That's a very unusual name," he says. "Of all of the names in the world, I wasn't expecting that!"

"Is it because it is 22 letters long, Felix?" asks Mom, counting the letters on her fingers.

I think for a minute, then I realize that I hadn't even counted it.

"Actually, I just thought it would be good to name her after two people who I really like and who have helped me a lot recently. Unless you'd prefer to call her Hugo?"

They both laugh. Dad nearly loses another mouthful of coffee.

"OK, Claudette-Charlottina it is," says Mom. "Although I can't help but feel like that is a bit of a mouthful. Can we maybe shorten it to something else for everyday use?"

"Like Claudie?" says Dad.

"Or Charlotte?" says Mom.

"What about Lottie?" says Dad.

"Or Tina?" says Mom

I stop and think for a moment.

"What about CC?" I say.

I say it again in my head. It is just two letters long, or technically it is the same letter twice. I like it.

"Welcome to the family, CC Twain," says Dad and we all know that it is just perfect.

Twenty-Seven

The next morning, before I can get out of bed, I decide to start a new morning ritual. I lie still with my eyes closed right until the very last minute. This is because if I open them, I might be tempted to count the slats of the bed before I can get up. It is a good feeling to be able to get out of bed and not worry about whether an even number or an odd number is going to be able to determine how my day goes.

I close my eyes and jump out of bed.

With Mom still at the hospital and Dad in charge, our morning at home is still mayhem. I manage to get myself some cereal. I still sit to eat in my spot with my bowl and my spoon. And I still like pouring the milk in as I go, but only because it means that the cereal doesn't go all soggy while you eat it.

When I get to school, the classroom is its usual hive of activity. Gerund and Oscar are having a paper plane flying competition with Greg and Andy as the official plane flight distance measurers.

Daisy, Maisie, and Samira Chen are sitting on their desks chatting and Alva is neatly writing reminders on the board.

Everything is pretty much the same as it always is, except that there is no Charlie to sit next to me. I'd become used to her sitting there, trying to borrow my pens all of the time. I lift the lid on her desk and inside it is empty. She really is gone.

Mrs. Green comes in. She is carrying a green piece of paper and when they see her, everyone scurries to take their place, ready to start the day.

"Felix," says Mrs. Green, looking at the paper. "I've got a note here that says Mrs. Lovejoy wants to see you in her office."

Everyone looks at me. There must be some mistake. I've only been at school about ten minutes. I haven't had a chance to do anything that would make Mrs. Lovejoy displeased with me. Then I remember about the other day, when I ran off to the library instead of going to the African music afternoon.

I take one last look around the classroom. It is going to be sad to leave Scribbly Gum. Will Mrs. Lovejoy let me come back and say goodbye to my class?

I drag my feet the whole way there, certain that I am about to be expelled. Goodbye, Scribbly Gum Primary School. Goodbye, lockers. Goodbye, monkey bars. Goodbye, comfy old log.

When I arrive at the office, Mrs. Troy seems a bit

nervous about the idea of me waiting inside Mrs. Lovejoy's office by myself, so instead she suggests that it might be better if I sit on a chair just outside and wait. Minutes later, Mrs. Lovejoy appears at the end of the hallway carrying a cup of tea.

"Felix," she says, when she sees me. "Come in."

I follow her into her office. It looks the same as when I was in here last time. Less wet perhaps and fewer feathers everywhere, but it is good to see that she has taken some of my decorating suggestions on board. There are still only four pictures framed behind her desk and only two bright cushions are sitting on her armchairs.

"Miss Claudette showed me what you did in the library the other day," Mrs. Lovejoy says.

"I was just having a bad day," I blurt out. "There were all of these problems and I didn't know how to solve them and I was overwhelmed and I couldn't stand up to Basil and please don't expel me, Mrs. Lovejoy."

I pause and gasp for breath. Then fall to my knees and clasp my hands in prayer position for dramatic effect.

"Expel you?" says Mrs. Lovejoy.

She looks confused.

"Is that why you think you're here? I'm not going to expel you, Felix. I asked Mrs. Green to send you in so I could commend you. I have noticed a real change in you lately and I was going to tell you that I am

impressed with how hard you have been working to improve your behavior. It certainly hasn't been perfect, but big changes like this take time."

Then she smiles at me from across her desk. Mrs. Lovejoy actually smiles a big, genuine proper smile at me.

"Plus, Miss Claudette said that she couldn't run the library without you and after seeing your work the other day, I can see why. You have a real eye for attention to detail, Felix."

I'm extremely surprised.

"Thank you, Mrs. Lovejoy," is all I manage to splutter in reply.

"Now, you'd better get back to class," she says, and I jump up and dash out of her office before she can change her mind.

On my way back to the classroom, I allow myself a quick stop off to see Hugo. He won't believe it when I tell him what Mrs. Lovejoy just said and I have something I want to give him.

I knock on the door to his room and when he doesn't answer, I open the door and go in. He isn't there and his room looks exactly the same as it always does.

I reach into my pocket and take out my pair of small wooden elephants, the one that still has four good legs and the one that is being held together with glue.

I put the elephants on his computer keyboard where he is sure to see them the next time he sits at his desk. Then I carefully take the note I have written and tape it onto the trunks of the elephants. It says:

Thank you for all of your help with Basil, Hugo (even though sometimes you had to be a bit mean to be helpful!). I am giving you these elephants from my collection, even though Mom thought I should throw the broken one away, because I know now that you don't have to be perfect to still be good. I will never forget your advice (just like elephants never forget. That's a fact!). From, Felix.

I arrive back to class in time for the second half of our math lesson. I'm surprised to find that someone has put a copy of the worksheet on my desk and that they have even written my name at the top in neat cursive script. When I don't understand how to do the questions, I can feel Basil begin to uncurl his leaves in my brain, but instead of giving in to him, I put up my hand and ask Mrs. Green for help. She explains it to me twice before I get the hang of it and manage to complete most of the page before the bell goes without any kind of major meltdown.

At break time, I sit down on my log and I'm about to take a bite of my apple, when Samira comes running over.

"Hey, Felix!" she says. "Want to play with us?"

I look over at the court. There is a large group already lined up under the hoop. They're ready to play.

"But even if it is just me?" I ask. "I mean, even without Charlie?"

Samira grins.

"Even if it is just you. Even without Charlie. You know, you're different than what you used to be like. Like you don't get upset so easily anymore. Like we don't always have to do things your way."

"I wasn't being difficult on purpose, you know," I say, walking beside her. "I just didn't know how to explain what was going on in my head."

"I know that now," says Samira. "We all know

that now. When you were away yesterday, Charlie explained everything."

"Everything?" I ask, trying not to sound alarmed. Samira laughs.

"Well probably not everything," she says. "Just enough to help us all to help you. We didn't really understand you that well before. We should have tried, though. Sorry."

I smile at her. "That's OK. I didn't really understand me that well before either."

She smiles back and throws me the ball.

"Ready?"

I nod and pass the ball to Tim who is waiting at the front of the line.

"Ready when you are."

Epilogue

Deer Felix,
Thank you four your letter. I'm pleazed to
hear that CC is doin well and that you have
startd her on comic books erly. Make sur you
get her Superman. He iz the best! Things ar
going well here. Ben iz gettin the help that he
needs and so am I. Thay ar giving me extra
reading and writin lessons at schoole. I'm not
perfect yet but I am improving. Don't you
think? Mom sold a huge wedding cake and has
bought a mooring permit four the boat, so we
ar gonna be here for a bit. You shuld come
and visit in the school holydays.
From Charlie

PS. Bee sure to Knockout that annoying Gerund O'Toole for me
next tim you ar playin Knockout!

Felix Twain
C/o Scribbly Gum
Primary School
Wattle Creek VIC
AUSTRALIA

About the Author

Sally Harris grew up in rural Australia and after graduating from Cambridge with a degree in Children's Literature, Sally has been busy writing, and working as a primary teacher in both Australia and the UK. Sally loves animals, including penguins, but as she can't have one of those as a pet, she has found that a dog is definitely the next best thing.

About the Illustrator

Maria Serrano was born in Murcia, Spain where she still lives and works. After completing her BA in Arts at Complutense University in Madrid, she went on to illustrate children's books for several Spanish publishers.